August

a novel

August
a novel

WILL OVERBY

BLACK CAT BOOKS

DAWSON SPRINGS, KENTUCKY
2012

Chapter 1

1

At first glance, plodding through the dusty green field in the yellow light of the velvet summer afternoon, her slim body clad in tight faded jeans and a worn t-shirt, Carla might have appeared lost. But she had been down to that tree by the Ashby River – her private place – and now her mind was fresh and clear. But she scanned the hazy, gray, dead horizon and thought, *I am a woman drifting through life. Drifting. . .*

She ducked through the barbed-wire fence and wound through the maze of corroded car parts that littered the lot behind the grubby white concrete-block building that served as a small grocery and garage. There was no grass back here behind the store, just gravel and dust blackened with motor oil. She caught her reflection in the grimy windshield of a junked 1973 Lincoln and pulled her tangled brown hair up, posing in the cracked glass. Not bad for an old woman of thirty-two. The grime on the window smudged the tiny wrinkles around her eyes, and she almost looked pretty. But the sun's glare pierced her eyes and she moved on.

Dan was changing the brittle, rusty spring on the screen door in front as she stepped around the corner. "Where've you been?" he asked with narrowed eyes.

"Took a walk down to the river." She knew it annoyed him when she left the store during the day, and she felt a thrill through her gut. It wasn't like they were swamped with customers; not that many people shopped at Turner's Gas & Groceries on lonely Highway 1348.

"The river," he said. "Why don't you just move down there? Just take all your shit and you can camp right by it. Plenty o' fish."

She took her seat on the stool behind the counter and watched the heat ripple up from the roadway. It was going to be hot this afternoon. *A scorcher* as they liked to say on TV. The Colonial Bread man would be here soon and he would be reeking of sweat and dirt. He would flirt with her and she would pretend to be interested in a fifty-year-old paunchy truck driver. On the small radio under the cigarette rack George Strait was crooning about Amarillo, and she wondered what Texas was like, if it was as hot and dusty as Kentucky in the dead of summer.

Dan gave the new spring a tug and let the door slam. He gathered his tools and headed out the side door to the garage. On his way past the counter he grabbed a snack cake off the rack. "Got a cupcake. Mark it up." She blew out a breath and pulled out a yellowed stenographer's pad where she kept track of their personal purchases from the store.

The bread truck pulled into the lot with a squeal of brakes. The driver swung out and started loading the dolly. His gray hair hung limply over his forehead and dark patches stained his shirt under the arms. Carla gripped the edge of the counter and forced a smile as he burst through the door with "Baby, I'm back!"

She clenched her jaw. "You sure are."

* * *

Above the store was a makeshift one-room residence. When she and Dan first married she called it a loft apartment, like people on TV had. She imagined dressing it up with screens and dividers and hanging colorful art on the walls. She envisioned parties with friends and serving drinks and tiny *hors d'oeuvres* on platters while soft music floated through the background. Now she just called it a room.

In one corner stood an old iron bed from her mother's attic; the mattress sagged and the springs were rusty and squeaky, but at least the sheets were clean – she always made sure of that.

In the other corner, past a row of three curtainless, multi-paned windows, sat the color TV, where Dan now sprawled in the ratty recliner watching *The Dukes of Hazzard*. The twenty-five-inch Zenith was new, bought on credit from Hayes Appliance Store in downtown Macon City. She supposed they would be paying fifteen dollars a week on it until they retired.

Over here, next to the kitchen/dining area where she now stood, was an added-on "bath" – a toilet, sink, and shower stall all in the corner, lit from above by a single bare bulb. There was no door, only a faded green curtain to be pulled around the open area for privacy. The commode was stained yellow, and now matter how hard she scrubbed she could never get the porcelain white.

The kitchen, if you could call it that, was crammed into this end of the place like an afterthought. Light came from a fluorescent fixture that she had installed herself over the kitchen sink. The table and chairs sat in the dead center of a gigantic, moth-eaten Oriental rug she had spotted at a flea market and persuaded Dan to splurge on. It was the only covering for the concrete floor.

She spooned macaroni and cheese onto a plate and topped it with a slice of French garlic bread. "It's ready," she said. She poured two cups of coffee and set them on the table.

He stood and shuffled over in sock-feet. As he sat, he took a sip of his steaming coffee and made a face, then turned his back to her to get a better view of the television.

They ate in silence as Sheriff Coltrane chased Bo and Luke Duke down a dirt road. The sheriff's car hit a tree and the General Lee sped off into the dust blaring its horn. Dan exploded with laughter and noodles flew out of his mouth. With oil-stained hands, he tore apart a slice of French garlic bread and wiped at the cheese on his plate, then crammed the whole mess into his gaping mouth.

Sickened, she scraped the remaining food off her plate into the garbage and let the dish clatter into the sink. She glanced down at the counter and noticed the light glistening on the wet blade of a butcher knife. She took hold of the smooth wooden handle and lifted the blade up before her face. She watched the beads of water race down to the silver point, then ran her thumb down the edge of the knife and relished the pain as a line of blood appeared. She walked toward him, the knife held out in her clenched fist, and brought the blade up to the nape of his freckled sunburned neck until it was almost touching the ends of his oily yellow hair. How she wanted to shove it in – to watch the knife slide through to come out his throat on the other side. How she would laugh as he choked and spurted blood all over his dinner, looking at her with a puzzled, idiotic stare.

She set the butcher knife on the plate in the sink. He was still engrossed in the TV. He hadn't even noticed her get up from the table.

* * *

Later that night, as a warm breeze stirred through the open windows into the darkness, he took her on the bed. He entered and the stench of sex and sweat flooded her nostrils, and she felt the vomit inch its way up her dry throat. She lay still as he pushed his dirty, sweaty body all over her, his breathing loud and anxious in her ear. She was relieved when he was finally moaning in his pleasure. She moaned with him although she felt nothing herself.

When he was finished, he kissed her neck and patted her on the cheek, then crawled off and made his way to the toilet. He pulled the dark curtain around the corner and a sliver of light spilled across the floor. She watched his shadow as he urinated loudly – like a horse, she thought. He started the shower, and as he stepped into the stall, she let out the breath she had been holding since he had begun.

* * *

In the morning Carla stood in the back yard hanging wet jeans, shirts, and underwear on the clothesline in the early yellow light. Her portable radio sat in the dewy grass, blasting the latest mindless rock songs. The disc jockey announced that it would be a gorgeous day. She doubted it; already rainclouds were blowing in from the West.

"Hey, Carla," a voice called to her. She looked up. It was L.D. Simpson from down the road. She smiled and waved.

He and Dan were soon discussing a set of old wheels. She watched them as she pinned a shirt to the line. L.D. was nice enough. Why couldn't she have married a man like him?

She turned back to the laundry. There was a comfort in the way the clothes rose and fell with the breeze, something lulling and beautiful.

Across the yard, Dan said something to L.D. and they both laughed. Were they talking about her? Her face burned red. She was pinning one of Dan's best shirts to the wire, and she imagined what it would feel like to rip the cloth with one of his razor blades – to sever the sleeves and pry off the buttons.

All men were the same. She watched Dan and L.D. and knew it was true.

2

Brian DeCanto thought: *Bitch.*

He peered out the grime-coated window at the filthy town of Cranston, Indiana, then let the curtain drop. He flopped down on the ratty motel bed. In one corner of the tiny room was almost everything he owned stuffed into two army-issue duffel bags. He sat up and reached over to click on the television. He lay back down and pretended to stare at the Olympic athletes rowing on a river somewhere around Los Angeles.

He didn't know what had happened. Cindy was special at first, not silly and giggly like all the girls he had known before. Something had clicked between them immediately. There had been magic. Making love to Cindy had been an experience in itself – she had known so much. Never in all of his thirty-six years had he ever met anyone quite like her: quiet, sophisticated, classy. She had been someone he felt proud to have on his arm when he walked into a place.

But then the fights began. Always something petty. She didn't like the way he hung up his towel. He left a dirty cup on the coffee table. His boots were in the way of the back door. Nothing he did was ever good enough. And then there was the fact that she thought he was screwing every girl he came in contact with. That fear of hers had led to a big blow-up last night. They had been out at a bar, laughing and having fun. But when the waitress dropped of their ticket she accidentally brushed her hand against his. Cindy's eyes immediately turned to fire. "Do you know her?" she said. He tried to reassure her that he'd never seen her before. But before they got outside, Cindy was accusing him of having a fling with the girl. By the time they got back to the apartment, she wasn't speaking to him. He had spent last night on the couch. But this morning they had made up, or so he had thought. When he came in from work all his stuff was packed and standing outside the door in the hall. He reached for his keys to let himself in and then made the discovery: she had taken the key to the apartment from the ring either last night or early this morning. Somehow that thought scared the shit out of him. He could see her standing over the bed in the darkness, grinning and staring down at his naked, vulnerable body while she slipped off the key and thought of doing God-only-knew what else. And then he became angry. Not just mad and hurt, but furious. She had known this morning it was going to happen. She had known as she fixed his morning cup of coffee; had known as she kissed him goodbye. And now, as he thought back on it, he could remember seeing something in her eyes that he hadn't understood then – a kind of guilt. And defiance.

But now that was the least of his worries. He had come back early to tell her that he had lost his job at the factory. That son-of-a-bitch foreman Robinson had never liked him, was always griping about little picky-assed things. Today it had been over Brian's parts reject rate. "Too fucking high," as Robinson put it. Brian told Robinson to go shove it up his mother's ass, and Robinson fired him on the spot. He had thought Robinson was joking at first, and he laughed. But Robinson hadn't been joking, and Brian had been given his final paycheck and a one-way ticket to unemployment.

When he had walked into the apartment house on Sims Street, he was so angry he was shaking. And then he found his bags.

He lay back on the bed and lit a cigarette. It had been one hell of a day. Tomorrow he would go down to the unemployment office. It would be at least a couple of weeks before his benefits started, but right now he still had money in his pocket. He had thought about escaping for a long time; maybe now he could take off for somewhere since nothing was holding him here. He took a long drag off the cigarette and stared at the ceiling. He could head down to the Gulf. Get himself a little place, maybe save up enough money for his own boat. He'd heard jobs were plentiful down there. Lots of construction going on. He hadn't worked construction for several years, but hell, it was just like riding a bike. All you had to do was get back on.

* * *

Around three o'clock he decided to get out and take a walk on the streets; there sure as hell wasn't anything for him in that room.

He trudged down the hot sidewalk, his wide muscled frame hulking past the bars and shops. He passed Carlton's Pub, a place he and Cindy frequented on weekends. He considered stopping in for a drink, but then thought better of it; he knew everyone in there too well, and they would ask about her. And he didn't feel like talking. But God, would a cold beer taste good right now. It was searing outside, and the hot air off the street buffeted his face like he was standing over a grill. Sweat flowed down his face in rivers, and his blue work shirt was itchy and sticking to his back and underarms. He decided he would take a detour into the next place that had neon in its window.

He stepped around the corner and stopped. The whole town lay spread out down the hill below him, an unsympathetic, bitter place. On the vague horizon, the steam from the power plant boiled upward to obliterate the sky. It was as if he could feel all the expectations and dreams of the people going up with the steam. A hard town, he found himself thinking.

Most of the men around here worked at either the factory or the plant. There just wasn't anything else unless you went south to Louisville or north to Indianapolis. But who wanted to do that? Most of these people's roots were here, and they had their homes and wives and kids here – their lives were all neatly arranged.

He had realized over the years that most everyone who was born here lived and died here. It was like a magnet. He wished he could tell that to all those young kids in Cranston High School. The town was a magnet, and if you allowed it to grab hold of you while you were young, you could never make it let go. You became damned. Anchored to the place. Chained to it. And the worst part was, once it got you, you didn't care.

But maybe he had found a way to escape it. Maybe if you just jumped into your pickup truck with everything you owned and drove away, not looking back. Maybe that was it – you had to do it, not think about it too much. Like a reflex.

He turned and made his way back toward the bars. He would get out of here, he decided. But there was something he had to do first, something that needed a lot contemplating. And it needed an ice-cold Budweiser to go with it.

3

Around the time that his father was in the process of firing Brian DeCanto, Shane Robinson had just settled onto his bike for the coast down the long driveway. He loved the way it felt: flying down toward the highway, bent over the handlebars, the roar of the wind in your ears becoming louder until it was all you could hear. Then the wind became your bicycle and you were floating on it.

At the edge of the road, he hung a tight right and headed down toward Tommy Ray's house. Tommy was his best friend even though he got mad over the littlest things. Once he had left Shane's house in a huff because Shane had found him so quickly in Hide-and-Seek. Stupid. But he was the only kid to play with out here in the damned country.

The day was bright and clear as he pedaled along the yellow line at the edge of the road. The sun was just beginning to dry the dew and burn off the morning haze as it streamed through the trees. It would be a fine day to ride bikes, he thought.

His mom had already yelled at him once today – about his room being messy. He hated her so much sometimes. And his dad, too. According to them, he was always dirty, or his clothes were ripped (from playing so hard, he supposed), or his room was a mess, or he was hateful, or he was spitting or picking his nose (well, at least he didn't eat the boogers like some kids in his class did), or he wasn't minding his manners like a good young man. Bugshit. Most of the time he thought they would be better off dead.

And that was the last thing he remembered. . .

. . . when he woke up in the weeds at the side of the highway. His arms and legs were wet and sticking to the dampness of the high grass. He had ridden right off the road into the field. His right leg was under the bike, bleeding where he had scraped his ankle on the pedal. His arm tingled, and he wondered if he had hit his funny bone in the crash. He sat up and his head swam in that weird way it did when this happened to him.

Shane carefully lifted the BMX racing bike off himself and climbed to his feet. There was a dull ache between his legs. The pad on the top tube probably had been the only thing that had saved his balls. He rolled the bicycle back up on the road, and watched the blue tires as he walked it along to make sure the wheels weren't bent.

He had been having these goddang blackouts for quite a while now. Sometimes he didn't go out, but just walked around, confused, not knowing where he was. And sometimes before he went out he could feel his body jerking, almost as if he were trembling from cold. And then he would drift off, as if he were going to sleep.

Once he had blacked out on the playground at school and had come to in the school nurse's office. That had really scared him. His teacher had been there, too, looking very worried. The nurse told her it was probably the heat – it happened to kids all the time. They would play too hard and then get over-heated and pass out. So he had been sent home with orders to stay indoors and rest. After that, he had been careful to not be too active during the summer for fear of having one of the spells again. But then he had had another while playing in the snow last winter. And now he didn't know what to think, except that he knew it wasn't the heat.

He hadn't told anyone about it; he was too scared. He figured they would slap him into the hospital and tell him he had cancer or something, and then he would die. It was much safer to just keep his mouth shut.

He wasn't the only one in the family who had been acting strange lately. His sheepdog, Bowser, was always lying around, looking like he had just come back from a funeral. He was beginning to worry. His dad had promised they would take Bowser to the vet when he got home from work. What if something was bad wrong with him? What if they had to put him to sleep?

He mounted the BMX to ride it, but then thought better of it. His head still felt funny, and he sure didn't want to fall off again. He wiped his face with the tail of his Ocean Pacific t-shirt, then turned around and headed back for home. Tommy could wait. Shane needed a big glass of Coke and a swim in the pool.

4

It was going to storm. A big one, too, by the looks of it. A streak of lightning illuminated the brewing clouds, making them look unreal – an illusion in a movie. Carla turned away from the window and crawled into bed with an old Stephen King paperback. She tried to concentrate on it, but there was no use pretending she was reading when she was really watching the lightning in the corner of her eye. She tossed the book to the floor when she realized she had read the same paragraph three times.

The weekends were always bad. Nothing on TV but reruns that weren't worth seeing again. She hated summer – the time change, the heat, the mosquitoes. But winter was even worse. With the snow there was hardly a chance to get out to walk down to Mama's or over to the river. She was stuck here in this place with Dan.

Another flash. She stared up, wild-eyed, and counted until the thunder came shaking the walls and rattling the window-panes. The storm was getting closer.

She glanced over at Dan. He sat in his recliner, a burning cigarette and a bottle of Jack Daniel's on the small round table beside him, a baseball game on the television. In the fog of the blue smoke, he picked up the bottle and took a swallow straight from the lip, then chased the drink with a drag from the cigarette. She wondered how she had ever thought of him as handsome. It was hard to think of him like that now – in fact, almost impossible.

The flare of light brought her fear back. She had been afraid of storms ever since lightning had struck old Aunt Tildy's house and burned it to the ground, Aunt Tildy and all. That had been a long, long time ago, though, and now she remembered it only as if she had dreamed the entire episode of the flames and huddled under a black umbrella with Mama while sirens screamed all around them.

Dan snapped off the television and stumbled over to the bed. He smelled of burnt tobacco and whiskey. He slipped off his jeans and turned out the light. Carla felt him easing into bed and braced herself for what she knew was coming: he wrapped his arm around her and held her breast. He did this every night. In the beginning it had been nice and comfortable. But now it nauseated her. It meant that he owned her. It all made sense in a way. You took the bull by the horns, the tiger by the tail, the man by the balls, and the woman by the breast.

But, as streaks of lightning battled in the heavens and the raindrops struck a rhythm against the glass – tonight, at least – she was grateful for his being there. It was comforting to lie against the broad expanse of him and sleep.

Chapter 2

1

"I can't take much more," Carla told her mother. She watched the plump, white-haired woman scuttle around the long, narrow kitchen, preparing for lunch.

"Take much more of what?"

"Of Dan. He's drivin' me crazy."

Her mother stopped and stared at her. "You an' Dan havin' prollems?"

Carla looked away and took a long sip of acidic coffee. "Aren't we always?"

Her mother clucked her tongue and went back to the business of slicing a tomato. "Seems to me like most of them prollems is in yer head."

Carla watched the blade move cleanly through the vegetable. Red juice crawled toward the edge of the counter. It would be like that to cut their throats, she thought. The knife would slice so easily and neatly.

"Just seems like husbands an' wives didn't have all these prollems 'til that ol' women's lib'ration came along," her mother went on.

Carla smiled and nodded. That was the best thing to do, really – just go along with them. Yeah. Sure. Whatever you say.

A thought crossed her mind: Was she going insane? Was she crazy? She pushed it out of her head. It was impossible. She had heard that if someone thought she was crazy, she wasn't. But that was probably a lie – or something she had made up in her head.

But why was everyone was against her? Maybe it was her body chemistry. Some people, she guessed, just weren't cut out to live around anyone else; they needed to live alone. Grow old alone and die alone – maybe that was what she needed.

She remembered one of her high school teachers telling her English class once, "Wouldn't it be strange if one day a big door opened in the sky and this booming voice said, 'You can all come out now – you've been in hell all your lives'?" Yeah. It would be strange all right – to everyone except her. She knew she was in hell.

She slammed the cup down on the table with a dull thud, sloshing lukewarm coffee out onto the vinyl placemat. She brushed past Mama toward the cock-eyed screen door. "'Bye."

Mama whirled around, a neatly floured fish in one hand and a greasy fork in the other. "Ain'tcha gonna stay fer dinner?"

"No." She let the door bang closed and headed toward the road. The heat pushed down on her shoulders like a weight and she was sweating before she reached the end of the driveway.

2

Martha Parker turned away from the door and stepped back to the stove. She laid the fish in the smoking skillet and watched it as it began to fry.

It was a shame how kids today treated their parents. When she had been a girl she wouldn't have dared to be hateful to her mother. Maybe Carla needed to have a tobacco stick laid across her hind-end. But when kids got as old as Carla, you at least expected them to be respectful.

When Carla had married Martha had been excited at the possibility of grandchildren. But then Carla and Dan had informed her that they had decided not to have kids – "On account of money," Carla said. "I think sometimes Dan just works it all away." Drinking it all away was more likely. Martha had liked that boy at first, but now she thought he was nothing more than a deadbeat bumming his way around from one half-assed job to another, like so many others around here. She was sure Carla knew it and probably regretted ever getting involved with him. But in Martha's day, a woman stood behind her husband and supported him in everything he did, whether she liked it or not. Whether she liked *him* or not.

But people today. . . Oh, the people. Martha was almost afraid to go out anymore. Last week she rode into town with Hazel Farris to see about some new shoes at the mall, and she had been appalled at the sight of painted-up young girls and greasy-looking boys holding hands and kissing right out in public. It was downright sickening. Those things were for after dark, at home, and for husbands and wives to do, not children. And just the other day Mabel Johnson had told her about a little boy being molested by a fourteen-year-old in the mall restroom. Thinking about that made her shaky and sick to her stomach. And if it were that bad in a little place like Macon City, she could just imagine what people did in the big cities.

God would punish them all one day, she thought firmly. Then they would see. But you couldn't tell them anything. Carla didn't even go to church anymore. That's why she wasn't happy. That was exactly it.

She stuck her fork into the fish to flip it again, and that was when the pain struck her. A full feeling, like somebody blowing up a balloon just below her breasts, and a cold stinging throb that raced up her left arm to her jaw. She let the fork drop into the skillet and began to sink to her knees. Faintly she thought, *The fish is burning and there's no one to turn it. No one at all.*

3

"Been to that damned crick again?" Dan said as Carla entered the store. It was a little cooler in here, but not much. The ceiling fans only seemed to stir the dusty heat around.

"I was at Mama's."

He grunted and headed out to the pumps as an old rusty Chevrolet Impala pulled in for gas. Through the cloudy, black film of coal soot and road dust on the plate-glass window, she watched him insert the nozzle into the car's gas tank and begin bullshitting with the customer.

And for the first time, she began to think about the pumps. All that gas beneath them. Enough to blow fucking Turner's Gas & Groceries straight to hell.

She could see it all now – Dan strapped to the steel pole that supported the peeling Esso sign; Carla spilling a trail of gasoline from the rusty pumps to the edge of the highway. Striking the match. Touching it to the spreading web of liquid.

That was when the phone rang, and she jumped as if a cannon had exploded beneath her. "Turner's," she said.

"Carla, I think you'd better get down here to yer mother's."

She recognized the voice – old Mrs. Farris, Mama's friend. Panic rose in her belly. "What is it?"

"I don't know. I came in and found her on the floor. I think she might be havin' a heart attack. Hurry up!"

"Oh, God!" Carla pressed the receiver close to her head. Mama. Her Mama.

* * *

They were pulling Carla out of her mother's door in the emergency room. She only caught a glimpse of Mama lying stark, gray, motionless among the crisp, white sheets. Mama in a hospital gown and with a plastic identification bracelet taped around her wrist. Mama connected to needles and tubes and machines. Mama in her gown, she thought, and an old children's rhyme began echoing insanely through her head:

Jenny in her shimmy-tail

Jenny in her gown
Jenny in her shimmy-tail
A-runnin' through the town

"Mama!" she gasped. Someone's hand grabbed her shoulder. She clawed at it with her fingernails and began kicking and punching at the faceless people that were forcing her into the hall. "I want to stay with her!" she screamed. "Goddammit! Let me in there!" She knew she was making a scene, but she didn't care. It was her mother.

She was pushed into the pale, sterile hallway, the door slammed in her face. She knew they were only trying to protect her from seeing all the things they would do to her – tear the linen garment from her to expose her sagging, wrinkled, colorless body; beat her chest; shock her with electric paddles. . .

She slumped down into one of the hard plastic contour chairs that clung to the wall. Mrs. Farris was there; she sat beside Carla and patted her on the shoulders, babbling on all the while about how lucky it had been that she, Mrs. Farris of all people, had happened along when she did.

Carla looked away, said nothing. She could still see Mama writhing on the kitchen floor in her blue cotton housedress, her hand spastically squeezing another floured fish. Mrs. Farris saying, "Hurry! Call an ambulance!" And her own emotionless voice – as if she were a stranger here, or watching the events unfold on *Trapper John, M.D.* or *St. Elsewhere* – saying, "No time. Help me get her to the truck and we'll take her ourselves." The eternal miles into town. All the questions thrown at her all at once. Then the stretcher. The oxygen mask.

There was a commotion at the end of the hallway. A group of nurses and med-techs flew by with a gurney. A small girl rode on it, her broken body masked in a cloak of blood. Her screams sliced through Carla's head like a knife, and she found herself almost wanting to jump up and grab hold of the child and choke her, to wrap her fingers around her throat which was gooey and grisly with congealing gore, to beat her small head against the steel rails of the stretcher until the screaming stopped. But she was wheeled into a closed room and her voice could be heard no more. God help that little girl, she thought to herself. God help me. She dropped her head and stared at the floor, ashamed.

She was still studying the tiles when the doctor's shiny black shoes slowly stepped into her field of vision. She looked up into his kind face. She found herself drawn to his eyes. Beautiful eyes, she thought.

"I'm sorry, Mrs. Turner," he said quietly. "We lost her."

Her Mama was dead.

4

He moved through the woods that surrounded Robinson's house. He was stalking, he thought, and it filled him with something half thrilling and half shameful. There was only himself, the velvet night with its cover of darkness and constant insect drone, and the forest through which he moved.

At sunset he had left the motel and had driven out Highway 27 toward the outskirts of town where Robinson's sprawling, two-story brick house rose on a hillside like a monolith. On his way he stopped and peeled a dead cat off the asphalt and dropped it in a paper sack. His plan was to stuff the cat, bag and all, into Robinson's mailbox, then head back into town before he could be seen. But as he slowed to a crawl in front of the house, he realized Robinson and his family were gone; not one single light burned in the house. And the garage door was open, a black, yawning hole inviting him in. Maybe a dead cat on the doorstep would make more of an impression.

He pulled onto a weedy dirt side road down from the house. He didn't want his truck seen sitting in Robinson's driveway. He would cut through the woods, leave the cat inside the garage and head back the way he had come. Sudden panic hit him. What was he doing? What if he got caught? But he allayed the fear with a swig from the flask of Heaven Hill he kept in the truck's glove compartment, then took another for good measure. He grabbed a flashlight from beneath the driver seat and he stepped out into the woods. The twilight was just reducing his vision to a hazy, grainy image, like a movie that had been underexposed.

Now, after slinking between the trees, he stood at the random edge of the wood that surrounded the house on three sides. It was so quiet. Not one car had whizzed by while he had been standing here. He thought about Cranston and its constant, unstoppable roar, and he decided that Robinson had been smart to build a house all the way out here in the solitude.

Probably had a pool, too. He turned his head and saw the tell-tale silhouette of a slide rising up behind a brick wall against the glowing purple of the sky. Yep.

He glanced at the highway then made for the black opening of the garage. He shined the flashlight around at Robinson's tools, garbage cans, work bench, his kid's bike, and the back door.

He started for it and felt his foot kick something. It was a dog's bowl. A big dog's bowl. He almost expected to find the name "Tiny" ludicrously scrawled on the green plastic. But whatever kind of monstrosity the Robinsons owned, it was apparently with them. He stood still for a moment. No muffled growls. No chilling, affirming clicks of claws on the concrete floor of the garage. Nothing.

He set the bag with the dead cat on the step and on an impulse turned the doorknob. The door swung open with a muffled groan. He looked at the open doorway. What the hell? He was staring into a dark laundry room. He could smell the light scent of detergent. Maybe he was wrong. Maybe someone was here. "Hello?" He stood still as stone and strained for the slightest noise. "Hello?" Nothing.

Now he felt stupid. What would he have said if someone had answered? *Just dropping by to say no hard feelings. Here's a gift.* He stifled a nervous giggle.

He shined the flashlight into the laundry room and played it over the stacks of folded shirts and underwear. Maybe Robinson needed a dead cat on top of his clean socks. He grabbed the bag and stepped into the Robinsons' laundry room, almost tripping over a bundle of sheets on the floor by the washing machine. He set the flashlight on the dryer and pulled the cat from the bag. It was stiff and flat and had the unmistakable odor of something that had been lying dead in the hot sun for a long time. He placed it on top of Robinson's boxers and wiped his hands on his jeans. There. Take that, asshole.

He directed the flashlight into the next room. Might as well see how the rich folks lived. The kitchen was spotless. Dishes from dinner were drying on the rack by the sink. Something on the table caught his eye. A note.

Mitch,

Gone to Carol's. If you need me her number is 555-8219.

Liz

In the living room stood a massive stone fireplace and an equally massive television. A leather recliner sat in the corner. Brian imagined Robinson kicked back here on Sunday afternoons, watching football and downing beer, and his stomach burned. It must be nice, he thought.

Above the mantle was a portrait of Robinson and his family. Robinson, with his bushy dark mustache and sallow expression sat next to a slim, blonde woman with chiseled features. He guessed that was Liz. Behind them stood a freckle-faced boy with an open, honest smile and a cowlick in his light hair. Nice family. He felt a stab of guilt at the thought of pacing uninvited around their home.

A door to the left of the fireplace led to a small study. There was an antique desk and shelves full of books, but he couldn't imagine Robinson spending much time in here. He played the beam of the flashlight over the titles. Lots of Nora Roberts and Danielle Steele. A few Stephen King. No doubt this was the wife's domain.

A set of carpeted stairs led to the second floor, where he found the boy's room. Posters of Joe Theismann and Cal Ripken, Jr. decorated the walls. A Santa Fe train sat silent on a circle of track in the floor. On the cluttered desk was a framed picture of the boy and Robinson. Brian picked it up. The boy was in a little league uniform, grinning broadly beneath his cap. Robinson knelt beside him in a coach's shirt, smiling open-mouthed and looking happier than Brian had ever seen him. Brian set the frame back down and eased out of the room.

Down the hall he found Robinson's bedroom. A heavy four-poster bed hulked in the gloom. He looked at it with its flowery bedspread and piles of pillows and tried to imagine Robinson having sex there. He tried to imagine him making love to the beautiful woman in the picture over the mantle and realized he couldn't do it. The Robinson that lived here beared no resemblance to the Robinson who fired him yesterday.

He started out, but a sudden urge guided him to the bedside table. In the drawer, sitting atop a jumble of papers was a revolver – a .38 Special. He played the light over it and watched the barrel gleam. He reached for it. It was heavy and solid. He held it for a long time, feeling the smooth handle in his grip. He should take it. Robinson owed him. Robinson owed him his ass. He started to slip it in his waistband and stopped. No. He wouldn't do it. Robinson had just done what he had to. And now Brian was free to go somewhere else and start over. Hell, he should be thanking him. Besides, the dead cat was enough.

The room suddenly flooded with light.

Brian whirled around.

Robinson stood in the doorway, his hand still on the switch. "DeCanto? What the fuck?"
His eyes grew wide and Brian realized he was staring at the gun in his hand.

Brian put his hands up. "Hey, no, you got the wrong idea."

"Like hell I do."

Brian's chest tightened up. "No, see – "

Robinson took a step toward him. "I got you now, you lazy bastard. Breaking and entering. Terroristic threatening."

"I ain't threatened nobody!" Brian moved toward the bed. "Look, I'm gonna put the gun down."

Robinson was still coming. "You're gonna have a long time to be lazy now, you fuck. Disgruntled employee, coming here to vandalize my house. Leave me a little *present.*" His gaze was black and piercing. "You steal anything?"

"No," Brian said. "The door was open – "

"So you just decided to come in and make yourself at home?"

Brian had backed away from Robinson, and now he was pinned against the bed and the side table. "I wasn't going to take anything. I swear. I was just going to leave the cat."

"Oh, save it," said Robinson. "Tell the sheriff when he gets here."

Brian's legs went numb. "Look, I'll just go. I won't bother you anymore. Let's just forget it happened. Don't call the sheriff."

"Already did," said Robinson. "He's on his way now."

"Just let me go and I promise you'll never see me again. I'm leaving Cranston anyway."

"Give me the gun."

Brian realized he was still holding the thirty-eight. He held it in front him, pointing it at Robinson. "Stay back."

Robinson snorted. "You ain't got the balls to shoot anybody."

Brian moved toward Robinson, and the other man backed up a step. "Just let me get out of here. Just let me leave." Brian could see the barrel of the pistol shaking. His grip was so tight he couldn't feel his fingers. He motioned with the gun. "Get over there. Out of the way."

But Robinson didn't back up any farther. He held his gaze steady with Brian's. And suddenly he had his hands wrapped around the pistol, trying to wrestle it out of Brian's grasp. Brian pulled back, afraid to let go. And it was only a split-second later, when the large man in front of him began to sink to the floor that Brian realized the pistol had gone off.

He watched, horrified, as Robinson writhed on the floor, the upper half of his button-down now soaked with dark blood. He could only stare at the contorted face, the clenched fists. Every muscle in Robinson's body seemed to tighten at the same time, then relax. Brian dropped beside him, but he didn't have to touch the man to know he was dead. Death was in Robinson's glazed eyes – hollow and accusing.

Brian felt the sick rising in him long before he vomited. And as he was throwing up, all he could think of was *Blood blood blood his blood is on me and I killed him I killed him Christ Almighty in Heaven I did.*

And when he had recovered, coughing and spitting and crying from the fear of what he was going to do, only then did he notice the boy staring at him. Robinson's boy. Set in that freckled face under a mop of sweaty blond hair, the steel-blue eyes looked at him, looked right through him. There was no hatred in the eyes, no sadness, no fright; they were dull and lifeless as those of the man on the floor. But as Brian rose to his feet and pointed the gun in the child's direction, the eyes became round and panicked. The boy began to scoot backwards on the floor.

Brian started toward him. "Come here. I won't hurt you." There was a quaver in his voice and he struggled to control it. "Stop moving."

The boy froze.

"Did he really call the sheriff?"

The boy nodded.

"What's your name?"

"Shane."

Brian moved closer. "How old are you, Shane?"

"Ten."

Brian leaned in and grabbed the boy's arm. Shane screamed. Brian pulled him up to his feet. "Shut up or I'll kill you, I swear I will," he barked. "Understand?"

The boy nodded. Silent tears began to spill down his cheeks.

Keeping a grip on Shane's arm, Brian led them down the hall and toward the stairs. He stopped, remembering the bowl he had kicked in the garage. The *big* bowl. "Where's your dog?"

"We – we had to take him to the vet. He's sick."

He pulled the boy through the rest of the house, out to the garage and into the sweet, summer night air. A light breeze cooled his body, and he realized he was coated in a layer of sweat. He ran the back of his hand over his face and felt three-day's worth of black beard-stubble; the roughness seemed to bring him back a little. He had never wanted a cigarette so badly in his life.

Robinson's GMC pickup sat in the drive, and for a brief moment, Brian thought of taking it. But he knew as soon as the man's body was discovered, someone would be looking for it.

"Come on," he told Shane as they headed for the woods. "We're goin' for a ride."

Chapter 3

1

"Get in," he said, opening the door of the truck. The boy stepped up and slid across the seat. Brian followed and took one last look around at the woods before he slammed the door. Every few seconds he spotted the green, eerie flash of a firefly in the darkness. He started the engine and eased back into the roadway, then flipped on the lights and headed back toward town.

Brian drove straight ahead, amazed at how much he was in control of himself. He had just killed a man and he was guiding the truck straight as an arrow. It had only been fifteen minutes but hours seemed to have passed since he had pumped that bullet into Robinson's chest. He glanced over at the kid, who was a statue, his eyes staring straight. Not crying now. No emotion at all.

And that was when the shakes hit him. Brian's whole body was trembling, drawing up. He pulled over to the side of the road and waited for the spell to pass.

His heart was hammering as if it would break his sternum. He closed his eyes and felt each pulse of blood through his veins. He took a deep breath and blew it out, fighting to control the pounding in his chest. A wave of nausea washed over him, and for a moment he thought he would be sick again. He swallowed hard and gripped the steering wheel until his fingers ached.

Shane began to whimper, and suddenly he burst out in deafening sobs that sliced into Brian's head. "Shut up!" he heard himself scream at the boy, but the voice seemed to belong to someone else. "Stop that goddamn crying or I'll blow your fucking head off!"

Shane cowered against the passenger door. His cries turned to snivels as he struggled to quiet himself.

After several minutes, Brian was able to pull back onto the road, and soon they were entering the commercial section of Cranston. He was relieved to see that this side of town was dead at this hour, but as they got farther into the city, toward the bars, there were more and more people along the streets, and he prayed no one would notice them.

He pulled into the parking lot of his motel, and Shane shot him an alarmed look. "Where are we?"

"My motel."

"Wh – what're we gonna do?"

"I'm gonna get all my stuff and we're getting the hell out of here." He slid out. "Come on. And remember, I still got the gun."

Inside, the boy did as he was told and watched from a corner while Brian threw his clothes back into the suitcases and gathered up the rest of his gear. "I gotta use the bathroom," Shane said.

Brian looked at him. "All right. Leave the door open." He eyed himself in the scratched mirror above the dresser as he changed out of his bloody clothes and tried not to listen to the boy in the bathroom. So pale – God, he was pale. And that made him think of Robinson's eyes, cold and lifeless.

Shane stepped through the door. "I'm through."

"Let's go."

"Where we goin'?"

Brian stood for a moment, thinking. "I don't know, but far from here."

2

Carla had no idea how long she had been awake. She knew she had slept a little because her head was thick and dull. She guessed it must be about two.

Dan lay beside her, snoring loudly. He mumbled something and rolled over, his back to her.

Now! She slipped out from beneath the sheet and made her way across the room to the kitchen, feeling her way through the dark. It was calling her, begging her; the knife was screaming at her.

She opened the drawer a crack and slid her hand inside. Her fingers touched the wood of the handle and she grabbed it. Right now she could do it. She could just stab him while he slept. It would be best this way, really; it would be over so much quicker. Then she could pack all her things and run down the stairs to the pickup and take off for somewhere – anywhere. It would all be over in five minutes.

She crept across the cold, concrete floor toward the bed. She was going to do it. She couldn't believe it – she was really going to do it this time.

For a moment she stopped in front of the open windows and stared out across the nighttime countryside. The trees on the horizon were black against the dark, dark blue of the star-peppered sky and a light breeze stirred through, caressing her face, bringing her the scent of pine.

She took a step toward him, the knife uplifted.

The bird startled her before she even realized she had heard it. It was a mourning dove, right outside the window, its low, sad voice crying to her in the night: *oo-OO. . . oo. . . oo. . . oooo. . .* And the knife fell to the floor with a metallic clatter.

"What's goin' on?" Dan's voice said in the darkness.

She knelt quickly and grabbed up the blade before he could see it gleaming in the patch of moonlight. "What?"

"What're you doin'?"

"Nothin'. Couldn't sleep." She forced herself to take slow, measured steps to the counter and silently lay the knife down. "I don't know what's wrong."

"I don't either, but you're keepin' me awake."

"Sorry." Carla made her way back to the corner and crawled into the bed. And as Dan held her in that way of his, she knew that sleep would not come on this night.

3

In the bed of the pickup, Shane Robinson also lay awake. His arms and legs were bound with rope and his head was pounding with a dull throb. He rolled onto his side on the bundle of sweaty-smelling clothes that was serving as a mattress. The man was asleep beside him. He didn't know where the gun was.

Two hours ago they had driven off the road around to the back of a huge, dilapidated barn that sat black and massive in the middle of a cornfield where the man informed him they would stay the night. He had tied Shane with the rope and arranged the clothes in the back of the truck. Then the man had burned the clothes he had been wearing earlier and they had settled down with the man keeping watch over him.

The scene at the house was playing over and over in Shane's mind – his father's chest exploding, the blood, the man vomiting, his dad on the floor. . . None of it seemed real – the ride, the barn, the pickup, the rope burns on his wrist – nothing.

He looked at the moon through the motionless leaves of the tree they were parked under – a perfectly round, silver ball suspended magically from the stars, its surface spotted with craters. His father had told him there was a man in the moon – something about how the dark patches formed a face. But Shane had never seen it, and he wondered if that was just another story grown-ups told kids. Like the summer before, when they had gone to California on vacation. They had stood on the balcony of their hotel room to watch the red-gold sunset over the Pacific, and his dad had said, "Watch the sun real close, Shane. When it hits the water, it'll hiss." Now he knew that wasn't true, and he supposed the same was true for the man in the moon. Just bugshit.

He wondered whether his mom was home by now and had found his father. He felt sorry for her because of what she would see and how she wouldn't know where he was. But he had seen the note on the table, so he knew at least she was safe. And if she was safe, she would be looking for him. The police would be looking for him.

Tears welled up in his eyes again, and he stopped them before they could take hold. The man beside him had just drawn in a sharp breath and had begun to stir.

4

Brian came awake with a jerk. Shit! He had dozed off while watching the boy. He turned quickly, shined the flashlight, and saw with relief that Shane still lay in the bed of the truck, watching him. "Damn," he muttered. He reached into his shirt pocket for a cigarette, realized he didn't have one, and slumped back against the cab. Every time he closed his eyes he saw Robinson's face – the frozen shocked expression, the open mouth. The eyes. He couldn't stop thinking about Robinson's eyes.

The air was thick and warm and moist tonight, like a jungle. The hot breeze rustled the cornstalks like sandpaper. He looked up at the full moon and a chill rippled through him.

Shane stared at him from where he cringed in the corner of the pickup bed. His eyes were round and bloodshot. "Don't be afraid," he told the boy. "I won't hurt you. I've barely even touched you, for chrissake." He sat up and felt a sudden rumbling in his belly. He shined the light on his watch. 1:45. He hadn't had anything to eat since just after noon. No wonder he was starving. He glanced at the boy. "You hungry?"

Shane nodded in the glare of the light.

"Me, too. Let's go find something to eat." He stood and gathered the pile of clothes together and stuffed them back into the suitcase. Shane sat up. "Put everything back into that bag, okay?"

Shane did as he was told, moving slowly with his bound hands. In the circle of faint light, DeCanto noticed a bruise on the boy's cheek. "What happened to your face? You get into a fight?"

"Bike wreck," Shane said. His voice was barely a whisper.

"Oh."

When the suitcases were full again, Brian lifted Shane out of the bed and set him in the cab. He fumbled for his keys and slid in beside him. "Now let's find some grub," he said, starting the Ford.

5

The restaurant was a Jerry's.

The man had taken the ropes off in the parking lot, and Shane had thought of running away then, but decided not to; after all, the man still had the gun.

They entered the foyer of the restaurant and the man bought a pack of Winstons from a vending machine. "What's your name?" Shane asked.

"Brian."

The restaurant was pretty crowded for such a late hour, Shane thought. It must be what his dad used to call the "bar crowd." They were all loud and boisterous and thick cigarette smoke wafted across the tables.

Brian found them a booth in a dark corner, and when they were seated, he leaned across the table and whispered in Shane's ear, "Just remember I got a gun in my pocket, so don't try anything stupid."

Shane nodded and pretended to study the menu the waitress laid out in front of him, but the lateness of the hour and the smoke from Brian's cigarette soon made his eyes sting until he could barely read the selections. He was brought crayons and a picture to color, but he laid them aside, too tired and hungry to be interested.

When the small, plump girl brought their food, she said, "Kinda late for a boy your age to be up, ain't it?"

He only looked at her and nodded, knowing that he had better keep his mouth shut. When she was gone, Brian gave him a tight-lipped smile. "Good boy," he said. Shane looked away and bit into his hamburger; it tasted like old shoe leather, but he ate all of it anyway to keep his stomach from rumbling. And by the time the waitress had brought the check, he was almost nodding off to sleep.

Brian paid, and they left and made their way around the big trucks that sat roaring and snoring in the restaurant parking lot in the night air that had turned chilly.

Shane crawled into the seat of Brian's pickup and slid over to the passenger side. Through his drowsiness, he was vaguely aware of Brian slamming the door and starting up the truck. He didn't put the ropes back on, he thought thickly.

And when he opened his eyes, it was daylight. They had just crossed over a huge bridge that spanned a wide, sluggish river and down into a flat dusty town that spread out on both sides of the four-lane in the bright haze. "Where are we?" he asked, and his voice was hoarse.

"Kentucky."

6

Secrets.

The August heat harbors many secrets.

It knows who has cheated and who has been faithful; who has laughed and who has cried; who has been content and who has been restless. And it will know more.

It knows that Carla Turner is repulsed by her husband and has been trying desperately to find the courage to kill him; that she wants to run away to find what little happiness she can; that she would almost rather die herself than live with him.

It knows that Mikey Wood (whom everyone talks of as being a Good Christian Boy and who made the state all-star basketball team three years in a row and who will graduate high school with a perfect 4.0) sometimes sneaks down to his basement to pop reds or blues, or to have sex with Joey Thomason, the little retarded boy from down the road.

It knows that Hank Russell is having an affair with a girl from town, and that when he tells his wife he is going out with Buddy Morris, he is really driving over to Betty James' to spend some time in her bed.

It knows that L.D. Simpson's body is being devoured inside by cancer and that he will die in a few short months. L.D. doesn't know this himself, however, because he is too afraid to go to the doctor about the bloody stools he has been having.

It knows that as a little girl Mabel Johnson fed rat poison to a kitten and sat motionless, watching as it lay convulsing and vomiting blood on her mother's sundrenched lawn one afternoon sixty-two summers ago.

It knows that Richard Blackwell, whom everyone pities because his wife, Judy, left him and hasn't been heard from in years, actually suspected Judy of having an affair and marked the soles of her Sunday shoes with chalk. And when he came home and found the marks worn away, he confronted her with it. And when she said she had been nowhere, he stabbed her fifty-six times with an ice pick and buried her under the foundation of his new tool shed.

It knows that when Buddy Morris is alone, he sometimes draws the curtains and stands naked in front of the bedroom mirror and slowly slides his wife's pantyhose up his legs and then puts on lipstick and eyeshadow and watches himself masturbate.

It knows that the reason sixteen-year-old Janet Miller accidentally flipped her motorcycle and killed herself was that she had just burned her leg with a joint.

The August heat holds many secrets. And it will soon hold more.

7

Dan hadn't said anything about the night before. Maybe he hadn't seen the knife. Maybe he had been too close to sleep to notice. Or maybe he had forgotten. Either way, he hadn't said anything.

Carla stepped toward the screen door and stared out at the confident breaking light of the morning . Another day. Another day in this place with him. She had planned to be far away by now.

Yesterday she had dug into the box of photographs she kept under the bed and had found snapshot of Mama. The picture had been taken one mellow summer afternoon two years ago. Mama was seated in a red metal lawn chair, looking off toward the horizon where the sky had just started to yellow with the lateness of the day. At her feet lay Charlie, a decrepit brown-and-white mutt that disappeared a few months later. Behind Mama sprawled the vast, rolling Kentucky countryside: bluc-green hills, the black smudge that was a tobacco barn and the majestic trees that surrounded it, and Mama's garden with its small, neat rows of indistinguishable vegetation. A picture of perfect serenity, she thought. She had taped the photograph to the cigarette rack by the cash register so she could stare at it all day.

And then, after supper last night, she had come out to the front porch to sit in the calm of the twilight. She had gazed up at the sky toward the scattering of stars, trying to remember the constellations she had once known. How many times had she looked at this sky? How many times had she watched the lights in the sky and made plans and dreamed of what she would be doing in five or ten years? She had taken a deep breath of the heavy night air and smelled the gas and oil that had been her life for so many years. But she had also caught the faint scent of honeysuckle as it had drifted by on a slight breeze. And it had taken her back.

She was fifteen again, lying on the grassy lawn behind Mama's house, in blue jeans and bare feet, staring up at the night sky. The stars were above her, the earth beneath her, the grass already wet with dew. The smell of honeysuckle and lilacs and grape vines clung heavily to the memory, tinting everything a soft violet. If she closed her eyes, she could hear the faint, steady, drowsy hum of the cicadas in the high oaks. It was a memory that filled her with hope.

But now Carla stepped back into the store and switched on the ceiling fans; they cooled the place only a little. And she knew that it would be hot today.

8

Shane was fully awake by the time they stopped for breakfast at a Hardee's drive-up window. He ate his bacon-and-egg biscuit as they rode down the highway. The food sat in his stomach like a stone, but at least it was food.

He crumpled the paper wrapper and let it fall into the floorboard, then leaned back and closed his eyes. Though the day was becoming hot, Brian insisted they keep the windows open instead of wasting gas on the air conditioner. So the wind whistled around Shane's face, blowing his hair and bringing him the summertime smells of exhaust and freshly-mown grass.

He glanced over at Brian and watched the man's black hair ruffling with the wind. The man was big, muscular. His biceps looked as large as Shane's thighs. Even if Shane tried to escape when Brian didn't have the gun, there was no way he could fight all that muscle. But if he could wait until Brian was asleep and then make a run for it. . . But most of the time Brian kept him close. There hadn't been an opportunity to be alone, to plan, to make a break for it.

He wondered about his mother again. He knew she was worried. Had she called the police? What would she do? But he tried not to think of her, to concentrate on the passing houses, because when he thought of her, he cried. And he didn't want to cry again in front of Brian. Not ever.

So he watched the unhurried miles pass by, long and tree-lined. Towns and gardens and homes with sunny, picture-perfect lawns and lazy, dozing dogs danced past. There were children on bicycles everywhere, shouting to each other and playing games, and Shane wished more than anything to be able to leap out and join them. An old couple – maybe a grandma and grandpa waiting for the little ones to drop by on their regular weekend visit – sat patiently under the spreading shade of a maple tree in their front yard; their eyes followed the blue Ford as it passed them by.

All of it was set to the music from the tinny AM radio in the dash. Country music. Deborah Allen, Lee Greenwood, George Strait – people he had never heard of. He knew Dolly Parton, though, and was glad when she came on. A country cross-over by Stevie Nicks was next, and that surprised him; he had always thought she was rock-and-roll.

When the stations faded out, signifying the distance they had come, Brian would move the dial until another swelled on strongly. They had just picked up a station in a place called Macon City, when Brian pointed to something beside the road. "Look."

The house was squalid and white, set off a little way from the highway. There was a wide, grassy, shaded yard and a jumble of vines that Shane recognized as a grape arbor – something his grandpa had. But the sign was what caught his attention:

HOUSE
FOR RENT
INQUIRE AT
TURNER'S GAS AND GROCERIES
1/4 MILE DOWN ROAD

Brian looked at him. "Let's check it out." He wheeled into the drive.

Chapter 4

1

They had been at the house for three days. It had belonged to Carla Turner's mother, and they were renting it furnished. Brian had introduced himself as Brian Hamby, just moving here temporarily with his son "Robby" after a nasty divorce from Robby's mother. He hoped nothing had aroused any doubt. He had no idea if news from Cranston, Indiana made it all the way to this southern point of Kentucky, but the Turners hadn't seemed suspicious or nosy. In fact, they hadn't been back around at all. And why would they? They had been paid a hundred in advance.

He and Shane had driven into town to buy some clothes for the boy. They had also picked up a couple of fans. The house had no air conditioning, and the humid Kentucky heat was brutal, even with all the windows open and a warm breeze flowing through. On impulse he bought a small black-and-white television. Reception was decent from the stations down in

Nashville, even with just the rabbit ears. He had watched the news religiously the past couple of nights, anxious for any word out of Cranston, but there had been nothing.

He had no idea what he would do with the boy. Daytime was easy, when they stayed in the airless living room together with the blaring television. But bathing had become an issue. The small, jumbled bathroom had a window that opened, and to make sure Shane didn't try to use it as a doorway to freedom, Brian had to stay with him while he used the old-fashioned claw-foot tub. Brian shaved while Shane bathed, and after, he tied the boy to the exposed sink pipes so he could take a bath himself. The lack of privacy was ridiculous; it was impossible to use the toilet alone. Then at night he tied Shane's arms and legs to the bed in the smaller bedroom. He was confident Shane couldn't pull free from the ropes, but he still slept lightly, keeping an ear out for any sounds of the boy trying to escape.

He knew he couldn't keep this up forever. He would have to get a job. He would need money. Dan Turner had said something about needing an extra mechanic at his garage, and Brian had always considered himself reasonably good at fixing cars. If Dan hired him on, Shane could stay at the store with Carla where Brian could keep an eye on him. But how long could they keep that up? Another week? Two? Wouldn't the Turners begin to wonder why the boy wasn't going to school?

He would never be able to get to the coast now, not with the boy. His dream of escaping to a better life was over. Everything was fucked. All because he had wanted to put a goddamned dead cat in Robinson's mailbox.

Shit.

2

Shane hated the house – mostly because Brian made him stay inside all day, probably because he knew Shane would try to escape if he were outdoors. He didn't know where he would go, though, if he managed to get away. He could go to the man and woman at the store and tell them everything, all about how Brian had killed Shane's father and then kidnapped Shane. But they might just think he was crazy – or worse, making it all up – and they would send him back to Brian. And there was no telling what Brian would do to him then. So Shane decided he would just wait.

The past few days in the house had seemed endless. All day they sat and watched the tiny television as it played its interminable collage of game shows, soap operas, cartoons, and old detective series. And news. Brian was always watching the news. Sometimes he would flip the channels and try to watch two or three newscasts at the same time, and Shane knew Brian was watching for a story about them.

It was almost impossible for Shane to stay quiet and still when the sun was beaming down outside, calling and calling him to come out and play. The restlessness was beginning to build up inside him, and at times Brian would have him stand in the middle of the floor and do jumping jacks until he had exhausted all his excess energy. He just didn't know how Brian could sit on that ratty old couch all day smoking cigarettes as he stared at the TV.

The second day of living in the house, they had sat out in the yard part of the afternoon, and that had been nice. Shane had pictured himself sitting on his front porch with Bowser, watching the cars and trucks pass by on the highway way down the hill, sipping an ice-cold Coke, and then taking a swim in the pool. But then he had opened his eyes and been jolted back to reality. He would have loved to climb among the vines of the arbor and smell the delicious, sweet aroma of ripening grapes, but Brian didn't trust him that far from the house.

The nights were worse. Brian made Shane take a bath every night, and that wouldn't have been so awful if Brian hadn't had to be in the bathroom with him to make sure he didn't escape through the window. It was embarrassing, being naked in from of a man he didn't know. And being tied to the bed at night, it was almost impossible to sleep. The heat was all but unbearable; the sweat of his arms and legs pooled under the ropes that held him, making him itch. And there was no way to scratch those itches without moving the ropes back and forth across his arms and legs, and that made him itch even more. Somehow, through sheer exhaustion, he managed to get to sleep. And in the morning, as he was just stirring into consciousness, he would find that the sweat now covered him in a cold, wet glaze, chilled by the fan.

Surely he wouldn't have to be here much longer. Each day he longed for a police car to turn into the driveway, for his mom and the police to get out; for the cops to take away Brian; for his mother to take him home to Bowser and his room and Tommy Ray. And every day he watched out the window for the car that never came, the policeman that never knocked on the door. And every day he prayed, *Please, God, please. I want to go home. Please.*

3

As the light began to dim on another day, Carla sat in the cool darkness of the upstairs on a window sill and stared out across the faded highway. The setting sun flared in the neighbors' windows, making them glow, making the houses seem alive.

But Carla was only staring at the scene, not really seeing it. She leaned back in the window frame, wiped the sweat from her forehead with her T-shirt sleeve, and took a long drink of iced-down RC Cola.

Three days before, the man and boy had come about Mama's house. Carla had been taking inventory of the Colonial Bread when the screen door creaked open and there they stood.

It would seem that someone as immune to excitement as Carla would have failed to recognize adventure in the form of a man, but she had noticed it the second her gaze fell on Brian Hamby. She had noticed it in his slim, muscular body that rippled beneath the tank-style T-shirt and old jeans that he wore. She had noticed it in his thick black hair; his narrow, piercing brown eyes; the dark beard stubble on his chin. And she had noticed it in his deep, velvet voice when he said, "We came about the house."

For a moment, Carla could not say a word. She just stood there – a pencil and clipboard in one hand and a loaf of king thin bread in the other. Noticing they were staring at her, she managed to say, "Would y'all like to see it?"

After Brian and Robby had introduced themselves, Carla took them down to the old house, stealing glances at Brian all the way: his strong, clefted chin, rounded nose, and deeply tanned skin. She showed them the home, opening closed doors and flipping lights on and off. And as she watched Brian walk around the bedroom, his boots clomping heavily, she felt that old, strange warmth between her legs – something she hadn't felt for so long. A warmth she had thought was only a memory. And when he said they would take the house, that had been all she wanted to hear.

And now she sat in the twilight that still entered her window, thinking, knowing he was there. She had seen the bedroom light burning last night. She could only think about how she had wanted to be there with him.

Dan would kill her if he knew. If he had known she was thinking of another man while he made love to her last night. . .

But Dan was gone tonight. He had driven into Macon City to see his friends at a bar.

And Carla's heart hammered against her chest as she realized what she needed. What she had to do.

Before she could stop herself, she grabbed her keys and felt her way down the back stairs, through the store to the outside. She locked the doors, then stepped down toward the road.

She walked blindly along the side of the highway. A car's headlights caught her for a moment, and she looked at the ground so the driver couldn't see the lust in her eyes.

A million things were flashing through her mind – What if Dan came home early to find her gone? What if Brian wasn't even home? What then? What if he *was* home? What about his son?

As she neared the ramshackle farmhouse, she fled for the cover of a patch of tall, overgrown weeds. As she hid behind them, grateful for the protection from the headlights, she felt startled insects hitting against her legs. She had to laugh. Here she was, a grown woman hiding in the bushes like a child.

The glow of the bedroom's overhead lamp shone through the open window and she could hear the faint, steady hum of a fan. Her sigh was a mixture of relief and panic – he was home.

Watching both the road and the windows, Carla ran for the side of the house. She leaned against the rough shingles and tried to catch her heaving breath. She could feel her pulse pounding in her throat. Then, slowly and deliberately, she stretched up to peer into the window. Nothing. The room was empty except for the furniture. An oscillating fan sat atop the chest of drawers. There was light coming from the bathroom window across the hall, and she could hear water running. Slowly, silently, she slid around the corner of the house until she was clutching the frame of the bathroom window. And she looked in.

Robby was bathing in the tub right in front of her. Carla stared past him at Brian, who was shaving at the sink, clad only in his blue jeans. She watched the wide, thick muscles work in his back with each stroke of his razor, and her heart pounded harder as that warmth suddenly came to life within her.

"I've been thinking," he said over the splashing Robby was making in the tub. "Maybe we ought to head on down south in a couple of weeks. What do you say?"

Robbie stared at the bath water. "I don't care."

Carla turned away. She could not let him leave. Not when she thought he was what she had been missing for so long. Not when she realized that she was surviving each day on the hope that he would come by the store.

But she could not talk to him tonight. Not now when she was so giddy with lust. She slumped to the ground, her fingernails digging into the peeling white paint of the window frame. "Not tonight," she whispered to herself, and her heartbeat slackened.

Besides, Dan would be home soon.

4

Now Brian was talking of going farther south – maybe to Florida, and Shane knew his mother would never find him there.

He was lying in bed, tied spread-eagle to the posts, and as he thought of going on down south, farther and farther away from home, tears stung his eyes. He didn't sob or heave; the tears just slid out of him, and at first, he was unaware he was crying.

He couldn't remember his father's face.

Suddenly, he hated everything at once. He hated this house. He hated Brian. He hated being tied and restless. And he hated his mother for not knowing where he was. But even though it had all been building up inside him for the past few days, even though he was crying harder, he didn't move; he was too afraid he would wake Brian.

And then, as quickly as the rage had hit him, it was gone. He knew what he had to do. It was so obvious and so simple that he wondered why he hadn't thought of it before. There was one way to escape – just one.

The only time he could do it was during his bath, while Brian was shaving. All Shane had to do was jump out of the tub and run for the door before Brian knew what was happening. And Shane knew he could make it – he was a good runner. And then, once he was outside, he would make for the nearest house, bypassing the Turners'. It was simple, but it was dangerous. He didn't know what would happen if Brian caught him. But it was a chance he had to take. If only he had thought of it tonight in the bathroom, he wouldn't have to wait until tomorrow night to carry it out.

With his mind spinning, acting out the plan again and again, dawn was creeping into the eastern sky before Shane finally fell asleep.

* * *

The next day seemed to last forever.

He knew he would try his escape that night, and that made him more hyperactive than normal. Brian noticed his agitation. "What's wrong with you today?" he asked during an old rerun of *Mannix*.

"I don't know," Shane lied. "Just bored, I guess."

That afternoon he and Brian did their laundry. There was an old washing machine in the house but no dryer. There was a clothesline stretched between two poles out in the yard but Brian couldn't find any pins. They drove up to the store to borrow some from Carla Turner and Shane noticed something pass between them when Carla gave Brian the denim bag of pins and their hands accidentally touched. There was a weird feeling in the air, a sudden, hushed silence as they looked at each other, as if an unspoken understanding were being communicated between them. Then Carla looked away and it was gone. Shane didn't like it at all; it made him feel weird.

Back at the house, they took the wet clothing outside and hung it on the line. It would have been a good opportunity to run, but Shane knew it would be better at night. Brian would have a harder time finding him in the dark. So he waited with difficulty. When the clothes were dry in a few hours, he helped Brian take them down and fold them. And then, after returning Carla's clothespins, it was time to settle down and watch television – show after show after show. The waiting was the worst part – not knowing whether he would succeed. He only hoped that if he failed and Brian killed him, he would do it quickly and get it over with.

It wasn't until the ten o'clock news went off and Brian said, "Bathtime!" that Shane got nervous. It was a sudden feeling, unexpected and sickening. He stood and made his way into the bathroom. His heart! It was pounding so hard and loud that he thought Brian might hear it.

He started the water in the rusty tub and began taking off his clothes, arranging them in a neat pile on the floor where he could grab them up quickly. Behind him, Brian took off his shirt and laid out his razor and shaving cream. "That Carla Turner's kinda pretty," he said.

"Yeah," Shane replied, stepping into the water. As soon as he was in the tub, he felt a sweat break out on his face. It would be good to run naked through the cool night air. He watched Brian lather up his face and pick up the razor.

Shane grabbed hold of the side of the tub and leaped over onto the floor.

5

Brian had just started a stroke with the razor when a tremendous thump behind him made him jump, causing him to slice into his cheek with the blade.

He whirled around, and he could only stare for a moment as the boy seized his clothes and headed out the bathroom door. Brian dropped the razor and lunged for Shane, throwing them both down on the floor. He grabbed one of Shane's legs and the boy began to struggle, kicking and trying to pull away. But Shane's body was slick and wet, and Brian felt him slipping out of his grip. The boy finally broke free, but he only got as far as the living room doorway before Brian tackled him, this time throwing his arms around Shane's torso and pulling him down. The slam of their bodies hitting the hardwood floor was thunderous, and Brian felt something pop in his shoulder. But Shane was still struggling. Brian turned him over and sat astride his chest. Shane began screaming. "Shut up!" Brian spat in the boy's face. He came close to punching the boy – so close, in fact, that he had already drawn his fist back – but he slapped him instead. Shane screamed louder. "Stop that goddamn screaming!" He slapped him again, harder this time, and Shane quieted to a whimper. "What the hell are you tryin' to do?" Brian shook him. "Don't you ever – *ever* – pull another stunt like that. Understand?" Shane nodded. His eyes were round and scared.

He pulled Shane up and led him to the small bedroom.

"Wh – what're you gonna do?"

Brian didn't answer him. He opened the bureau drawer and threw a pair of underwear at the boy. "Put those on." Shane did as he was told, and Brian tied him to the bed.

"Brian? Are. . . are you gonna kill me?"

Brian looked at him, and he felt sick and perverted. Brian had done this. All of it. He had tied the ropes, had left the red handprint across Shane's cheeks. He had killed a man, kidnapped a child, stolen a gun. . . Hell, there was no telling what was going to happen next.

Are you gonna kill me?

Brian looked at Shane long and hard. "Go to sleep."

He shut the bedroom door and rambled back to the bathroom. Shane's clothes lay strung out on the floor where he had dropped them. Brian left them. Who cared? He turned off the water in the tub and let it drain out. He picked up the razor to finish his shave and then laid it back down. Fuck it. He reached for a towel and wiped the shaving cream off his face. The blood that had mixed with the lather had taken on an unnatural fluorescent pink color. He wet a corner of the towel and gingerly wiped at the cut. It was still seeping blood. He pulled off a corner of toilet paper and stuck to it.

Minutes later when he was in bed, he thought of Shane tied in the next room. He thought of the fear in the boy's eyes when Brian had him pinned to the floor.

Brian? Are. . . are you gonna kill me?

What a crock of shit. There was no way he would hurt that boy. He had never before wanted to be a father – the thought of such responsibility had scared him to death. But he found himself wondering how things would be if he really did have a child. He thought of having a real son and how they could go fishing and hunting together.

He hated the way he had treated Shane . He knew he couldn't let him escape, but he hated the fact he had struck him. A memory of his father nagged at him. The worst memory of his life.

His father had always been kind and fair, a loving man. Brian remembered the many nights he and his older brother, David, would talk to their father after dinner as they sat in the den. He couldn't actually remember any of the conversations, but he knew how he had felt then: warm and safe, the way he always felt around his dad.

But one night Joseph DeCanto was on whiskey, something he had never been able to handle very well. And eight-year-old Brian had an accident right in front of him. He had been walking through the room with a glass of Coke – something usually forbidden in the den but allowed on this one night as they watched the first game of the World Series. The glass just slipped out of his hand. It was as though someone had yanked the Coke right out of his hand and thrown it to the floor.

And then his father raised hell. He jerked Brian out from the middle of the mess and started shaking him – shaking and shaking until Brian felt as though he were on a ride at the carnival. And then his father had led him to the closet.

The closet had always been Joseph DeCanto's favorite method of punishment. He would put Brian or David inside for an hour or two, and that was usually all that was necessary to lead them back to the straight and narrow.

Brian would never forget that place. It was a world of utter darkness except for a crack of light that seeped in between the door and the floor. He had never been afraid of the dark, but it was different in the closet, as if the darkness had turned against him. Part of it was that the place was also the means of entry into the attic. He had only been up there once in his life, with his mother, and they had found a dead bat still clinging to one of the rafters, now gray and mummified. He had touched it and it had fallen right on top of him. He had screamed, thinking the thing had come back to life and was trying to kill him. From then on, his fears of the closet centered around bats swooping down from the attic and attacking him, chewing out his eyes, tangling in his hair. He had awakened more than once from a nightmare about that. But perhaps the worst part of being in the closet was the smell. Like something had crawled up in the corner and died. They had never known what caused the stink. David told him that he thought maybe a snake had slithered into the place and died in the wall, and that had been too much for Brian; he would never again sit on the floor or touch the walls of the closet. When the acrid smell became too much, he always buried his face in his father's worn work coats. The scent they gave off was of stale sweat and old cigarette smoke – a masculine, father-smell – but that was better than inhaling death. Somehow, never knowing what the smell was made being in the closet worse.

And on the day of the Coke accident, all his fears of the closet filled his head, and he panicked, thinking of bats and snakes and that horrible smell. And when he refused to go in, his father punched him in the face and threw him in. After that, even though his father sobered up and desperately apologized, Brian never forgave him for it. The only good that came out of it was that his father never used the closet as punishment again.

And now, after what he had done to Shane, Brian couldn't help but be angry at himself. He could see so much of his father in the way he had handled the boy. But the boy had to know that Brian meant business. And letting his guard down was not a risk Brian could afford to take again.

* * *

That night, when Brian finally slept, he dreamed.

He was in the closet; the smell was there, and the coats and the darkness. But something else was with him, something he couldn't see. And only when it fell from the top of the closet and landed on his shoulders, around his neck, did he realize that it was a snake.

For the first time in his life, Brian DeCanto woke himself up screaming.

6

When the man's scream echoed through the house, Shane came awake instantly.

The room was still hot as a greenhouse, stuffy and humid. Sweat was pouring off his face, trickling into his eyes, but there was no way he could wipe it off with his hands tied to the bedposts. He squinched his eyes shut as tight as possible, trying to squeeze the sweat out, but it only seemed to make it worse. It had taken forever for the sting to leave his face after Brian had slapped him. He had been crying ever since he had been put in here and he didn't care anymore if Brian heard him or not.

He stared at the ceiling and wished desperately that he could go back to sleep. Before, it almost hadn't mattered what happened to him, whether he lived or died. But now he knew more than anything that he wanted to be home again – to sleep in his own bed and be with Bowser and his mother, and most of all, to have these ropes off him.

He had never hated anyone as much as he hated Brian.

Chapter 5

1

It had been a hell of a night, first with Shane and then that damned nightmare, and sleep had evaded him for a long time. He could tell he was awfully tired – the inside of his head felt thick and fuzzy. He wanted badly to just go back to sleep, but he knew if he did he would feel sick when he finally got up. Besides, he had to feed Shane.

He dragged himself out of the bed and stepped across the hall to the bathroom. He urinated, then washed his hands while he watched himself in the mirror. He really wasn't a bad-looking guy, except for that crust of blood on his cheek from last night. He drew himself up and puffed out his chest, then flexed his arm muscles. Not bad. His black hair stuck up in tufts all over his head like some of those punks that used to hang around the pool hall in Cranston, but it wasn't thinning. And he knew his dark eyes were magic; they had worked on more than one woman in his lifetime. Maybe it was time for him to take a trip up to Turners'. He needed some relief, and Carla Turner seemed like she could give it to him. He knew he attracted her – he had seen it yesterday at the store, the way she had smiled at him, the way she had bitten her lip as he had smiled back. Yeah, they could certainly have a nice time together. There was something about her that was more than just the way she looked – all soft and fragile yet strong; slender but not skinny. More than the way her hair always looked wind-blown, something that was somehow flattering to her. The way her small, pointed breasts sat against her T-shirts. Maybe it was her maturity. Or maybe it was the way she exuded a natural, albeit innocent, aura of sexuality. Yeah. That was it, all right.

But Dan worried him. He was always there, watching everything with his cold eyes. There was no way Brian and Carla could fool around near the store. But maybe if he brought her down here to the house, Dan would never know. He could just tell them that he needed her to show him something about the house. But he would have to keep the boy out of the way, and he couldn't very well invite Carla into the house while Shane was tied up in his room. He would have to gag him, and he wasn't going to do that. He was horny but he wasn't cruel.

Then he remembered the little storage building right behind the house. He could fix up some kind of makeshift bed in there for them, maybe a mattress from the spare room. That way Carla would never even be in the house, and she wouldn't hear if the boy decided to make some noise.

Back in the bedroom Brian pulled on his jeans and slid into a T-shirt and his boots and headed for the back door. Outside, the morning was clean and fresh, and stepping into it was like being renewed for another day. He headed for the arbor and pulled off a stem of grapes, then made his way to the outbuilding.

He scraped the filth off the window and peered in. He saw with disappointment that the place was pretty nasty inside. No way. Dirt covered the floor and walls of the building like a carpet, and in the middle of the room lay a dead mouse. Not exactly the ideal retreat for lovers.

He popped a grape into his mouth on the way back to the house. There had to be somewhere he and Carla could go to be alone.

Inside he picked up Shane's clothes and headed for his room. "Wake up," he said as he opened the door. Shane lay on the bed, staring at him with intense hatred. "I brought your clothes." The boy said nothing and looked away. Brian piled the things on the edge of the bed as he knelt. "I'm gonna untie you so you can get dressed and eat."

"It's hot in here," Shane said, his voice hoarse.

Brian looked at him while he worked on the ropes, at the puffy face and red eyes, the sweat-soaked hair. "I know. There's nothin' else I can do with you right now."

"You can let me outa here."

"No sir. Not yet. Not after last night."

"Please?" the boy whined. "I promise I won't run away again. I promise."

"Forget it." Brian finally had the boy's arms free, and he handed him his clothes. "This afternoon I'll let you out but not right now."

"Why not?" Shane asked as he pulled on his Van Halen t-shirt.

Brian knew he couldn't tell him he was leaving the house for awhile, or the boy might try something else. "I just can't." He stood and aimed the fan squarely at the bed. "That'll help with the heat." He sat back down and unknotted the rope on the boy's feet. "There. Get dressed and come eat some breakfast." Brian bit a grape off the stem in his hand and looked right into the boy's eyes. "I don't want hear anything out of you," he said. "If you so much as make a squeak, I'm coming in here and beating the living shit out of you. Understand?"

Shane nodded and stepped into his Levi's. "I have to pee."

Brian led him to the back part of the house and stood just outside the bathroom door while the boy went in. "I don't wanna hurt you," he said. "But last night I had to show you that I mean business. You can't leave, and I'll do whatever it takes to stop you if you try."

The boy said nothing until he emerged from the bathroom. "Brian?"

"Yeah?"

"I hate you." He brushed past and headed to the kitchen.

Brian stared after him and pulled off a grape. He started to say something and then stopped, eating the grape instead. Little asshole.

They sat at the kitchen table while Shane ate his frosted flakes. Neither of them spoke. Brian lit a cigarette and took a long drag off of it. A hot breeze was stirring outside, and the birds were rustling through the trees.

He knew the boy hated him. He didn't blame him. Right now he didn't even like himself. He had no idea what they were going to do or where they would go once they left here. Part of him wondered whether he should have just offed the boy the night he shot Robinson. It would have made things a hell of a lot easier. But as soon as that thought hit his brain he shoved it aside. Robinson's death had been an accident. An *accident*. He had to remember that. Shooting Shane would have been nothing but cold-blooded murder.

When Shane finished his cereal, he put his bowl in the sink and Brian led him back to his room. Brian retied the ropes on Shane's wrists and ankles. "You be a good boy and I'll let you loose at lunch." Shane said nothing and stared at the open window. Brian looked at him for a moment and headed toward the hallway. He started to close the door, but decided leaving it open might keep the room a little cooler.

In the living room he flipped on the TV and turned up the volume just loud enough that Shane would be able to hear it. Then he slipped through the kitchen door to the outside. He would have to walk to the store or Shane would hear the pickup, but he didn't care; the day was only starting to get warm.

2

Carla had been thinking of Brian all morning, so when he walked into the store out of the dusty sunlight, she wasn't certain whether he was real or part of her fantasy. But when he spoke to her, she knew he was really there, and it made her laugh to think she had been so foolish.

"How you doing?" he asked.

"Fine," she answered. "What'cha need?"

"Nothing really. Just thought I'd come by and see you."

"What happened to your face?"

He touched the scab on his cheek. "Cut myself shaving. It's nothing."

"Where's Robby?" She peered past Brian toward the outside.

"I left him back at the house watching cartoons."

"He seems like a nice kid."

"He is. He's real good for his age."

The creak of the screen door startled her momentarily, and she felt a stab of panic when she saw Dan's stern face.

"Hey, Dan," Brian said.

Dan nodded at him. "Brian." Then he looked at Carla, and she saw the momentary flash of anger and jealousy in his eyes before he spoke. "Hank Russell called while ago when you were gone," he said, and Carla cringed, thinking he might ridicule her in front of Brian for going to the river. But he didn't. "He needs me to go look at his car – he can't get it started. You can handle it here for awhile, can't you?"

"Yes."

Dan glanced at the two of them once more and turned to go. They heard Dan's truck pull out of the lot and Carla felt her body relax.

"What's wrong with him?" Brian asked.

"I don't know," she said, and knew it was the truth.

Brian straightened. "I'm sorry – I didn't mean to pry."

"Oh, that's all right. No use pretendin' things are still okay between us." She looked back at him. "You still lookin' for work?" she asked quickly.

"Yep. You think there's anything around here I can do?'

"You mean here at the store?"

"Yeah. Dan said something the other day about needing an extra hand in the garage."

"You should've asked him about it just now. I'll bet you're real good with cars." And she blushed, remembering she had heard him talk about working on cars the other night when she had been peeking into his windows. "You can talk to him when he gets back."

"I will," he said.

"Oh, and I heard rumors that mine near Masonville's gonna hire about twenty men here pretty soon."

"Really? I'll have to see about that."

She shrugged. "Just a rumor."

The phone rang, and she answered it, irritated at the interruption. It was Hank Russell, looking for Dan. He talked on and on, even after she told him Dan was gone, and she listened while watching Brian pace around the store smoking his cigarette. When she finally hung up, she looked at Brian and gave him an apologetic smile. "I hate talkin' on the phone," she said. "And we only have the one. It was always a hassle when Mama used to call at night and I had to come downstairs and answer it."

"You don't have a phone upstairs?"

"No. Dan doesn't want the expense." She sighed and looked out the window. She was trying to think of something – anything to keep him here talking to her. She watched the warm breeze rustle the trees across the road and said, "I don't like summer much."

Brian grunted. "I do. I like it hot."

"Then you'll really like it around here," she laughed. "Last summer we broke all kinds of heat records."

The screen door creaked open and both of them looked up to see a round, red-haired boy step in and make his way to the freezer. The Miller boy, Carla recognized at once. He was covered with so many summertime freckles that it was hard to see the color of his skin. "Hi, Charlie," she said.

"Hi, Miz Turner," he said. He laid a Nutty Buddy and seventy-five cents on the counter.

"How's your folks?" she asked, ringing up his purchase and giving him his change.

"They're all right," he said. He took his ice cream and headed outside. "See ya later."

Carla and Brian watched as the boy, with his red hair and his equally red dog, started off down the highway.

"Who's that?" Brian asked.

"Charlie Miller."

"Not a very happy kid, is he?"

"He don't say much lately," Carla told him, her voice softening. "His sister, Janet, got killed about a month-and-a-half ago. Motorcycle accident."

"Hm."

"She was only sixteen."

"That's bad."

"Yeah." She looked around toward the refrigerated case. "Would you like a beer? I can give you one on the house if you do."

"Little early for a beer."

She felt her face turn to fire. "Of course. Of course it is."

He turned to the refrigerator behind him and pulled out a bottle. "I'll take a Coke, though." He winked at her. "I'll pay for it, too."

He gave her a dollar and she rang up the sale and slid his change across the counter. She was terrified to touch his hand, as if he could read her mind if they made contact.

He popped off the cap and took a swig. "So, you two own this place?"

"Yeah," she said and thought of the garden of junk outside. "It ain't much, but it's okay." Her eyes began to wander down his body to where black hairs were peeking over his shirt collar, and that nervous warmth returned. "Dan – Dan's been talkin' about movin' someday, but I doubt if we ever do. This place is paid for, and it ain't too bad," she said, trying to make herself believe it. But the memory of a few days ago came flooding back – the memory of holding the cold, wet knife to her husband's neck. "It's not bad at all."

"How come you didn't move into your mother's house?" Brian asked and turned the bottle up again.

"Dan," she said, and her voice sounded more bitter than she meant for it to. "He says it's like takin' charity. He won't live in a place he didn't pay for himself. Ain't that stupid?"

Brian grunted, an answer that could have been "yes" or "no." He lit a cigarette and offered her one, but she declined. "This all you do, run the store?" he asked, shoving the lighter in his pocket.

"Yeah." She fingered the edge of the worn counter and slid an ashtray toward him. "Dan don't want me to get a real job."

"I'd call this a real job."

She smiled, but couldn't bring herself to meet his gaze. "I guess."

"Does he do anything else? Besides this place, I mean?"

"Oh, he piddles around in farmin' some, does haulin' jobs for people, stuff like that."

The glow on the end of Brian's cigarette flared lazily as he sucked the filter. "Oh." The smoke crept out of his nostrils and curled its way up to the ceiling.

"So, tell me some more about yourself," she said. "Where y'all from?"

"Indiana."

"Yeah, I noticed the plates on your truck."

"Me an' Robby's mom got a divorce not too long ago, and I got custody of him. I thought this summer we'd just travel around, see where we wound up."

"Sounds like fun," she said, watching him take another gulp of Coke. "Think you'll stay around here for awhile?"

"I don't know." He smiled at her. "You want us to?"

"Yeah," she said, and her heart began to pound. "I – I like you – a lot." She laughed. "God. That sounded like somethin' a teenager would say." She blushed and looked away.

She jumped as his large hand settled over hers. She looked at him, and he was staring at her, his eyes black. "You know," he told her, "you are a very beautiful woman, Carla."

She felt her face turn hot. "Oh." She laughed, embarrassed. "Thank you, but – "

"No, I mean it. I've thought that from the minute I first saw you." She looked at him and realized what he was saying. Her heart raced as he reached out to cup her face in his hand. She felt the gentleness of him as he stroked her cheek and lips with his thumb. And suddenly, he had her in his arms, and there was an unending, clumsy silence before she finally felt his lips touching hers. Panic hit her, and she pulled away. "No – I can't." She met his puzzled stare. "I – don't want to."

"Yes you do," he told her, and she knew he was right. He kissed her again, and this time she kissed back, her tongue entering, probing, withdrawing.

She pulled back. "No. Not here."

"Where then?"

"Come on," she said, pulling him toward the front door. "I know a place."

3

Shane didn't know whether he had blacked out or just fallen back asleep, but the way the walls seemed to melt and tilt made him think he'd had another one of his spells. He watched the blades of the fan for a minute, but then he started to feel queasy, like that bowl of Frosted Flakes would come back up. He finally closed his eyes, and that seemed to help a little.

Beyond the door, the television continued to drone on and on, a liquid, indistinguishable, constant noise. He hadn't heard anything out of the man, though, and now he wondered if Brian was asleep or something.

Earlier he had tried twisting his hands around in the ropes to see if he could slip out, but it was no use. Brian had tied them good and tight as usual.

And now, as his head swam and his stomach knotted up, he began to cry again. He was scared the man would beat him again or do something worse to him. His parents had always warned him about strangers who sold children or took naked pictures of them doing nasty things, and he wondered if that was what Brian was planning to do.

Then he thought of Bowser. For the first time, he wondered how sick Bowser had been the night he and his dad had taken the dog to the vet. Dr. McGregor had wanted to keep Bowser at the clinic for awhile to run some tests on him, and he had said they would know something in two days. What if Bowser were dead now? Shane wouldn't even know it.

Sweat broke out across his forehead, and he continued to cry. But silently, so Brian couldn't hear him.

4

Carla had led him to a tree by the creek bank, and when he looked at her questioningly, she said simply, "Don't worry. I come here all the time."

They moved slowly at first. Brian undressed her and she did the same to him. They stood locked in an embrace forever, Brian tracing the curves of her with his fingers, exploring the dips and rises, the smoothness, the dryness and wetness of her. He felt her stomach press against him as he rose, and he could stand it no longer. They lay down among their clothes, feeling, caressing, tasting. Moments later, with her beneath him, he looked at her and thought she was the most beautiful woman he had ever seen. His movements became faster and faster. She stroked the arch of his back as it rose and fell, rose and fell, and suddenly she grasped his buttocks and pulled him deep within her, deeper than he had ever been, and she began to moan, her body trembling. And when Brian could take the beautiful agony no longer, he lowered himself to her and all the tired, restless ache exploded out of him.

5

Carla was relieved to find that Dan was still gone when she returned home. Good. Now she would have time to clean up before he got back.

She ran upstairs and jumped into the shower. Under the hot, sensuous water she picked up the soap and lathered her body, rinsed, then did it again. It seemed foolish to take two showers, but she wanted to get all of Brian's smell off her before Dan could notice it.

It had been so wonderful, being with Brian. After Dan, she had never thought she would enjoy making love to any man, but Brian showed her she had been wrong. He was only the second one, but she knew she could never be satisfied with anyone else. He had been so gentle and slow and caring. Nothing like Dan.

As she thought of the man she had just made love to, then man she had just taken inside of her, she felt that warmth again. She moved to touch herself, but then stopped. There wasn't time. Dan would be back shortly, and she didn't want him to catch her out of the store.

She stepped out of the stall and dried off, then pulled on her old clothes. She just hoped she hadn't taken too long in the shower.

She moved quietly down the stairs to the store and was relieved to see Dan's silver Bronco just pulling into the lot outside. She hurriedly took her place behind the counter and waited for him.

He burst through the door, his clothes and arms black and greasy. "Got that'n done."

"How much you make?" she asked him, knowing he would be pleased that she had taken an interest.

"Thirty-five." He pulled a Diet Rite out of the drink case and pried the cap off. He took a long swig and blew out a breath. "Mark it up," he said, holding up the bottle.

"What was wrong with Hank's car?"

Dan didn't answer. He was staring at her. He moved toward the counter. "Why is your hair wet?"

Carla felt the breath catch in her throat; she had forgotten to dry her hair. She reached up and touched it, smoothing it down. "I – well. . . it – it was hot and I thought that if I rinsed my hair I'd feel cooler, so I went outside and wet it with the hose."

"Hm," he grunted, and she was relieved when he turned away, sipping his cola and looking outside at the hazy landscape. "I don't know what I'm gonna do about all this backlog of cars needin' to be fixed. Hank's was the third one today. I ain't got time to run all over the country and run this place both."

"What about that Hamby man?" she said. "When he was in here he said he was pretty good with cars, and you know how bad he needs a job, with that boy and all. You could let him take care of the garage while you do all your runnin' around."

Dan looked at her. "Yeah," he said. "That's not a bad idea. I'll think about it." He took a sip of his Diet Rite. "Can't pay 'im much, though." He drained the bottle and slid it into the rack of empties. "Be a load offa me, that's for sure." He stepped out onto the front porch, letting the screen door bag against the frame and pulling on his cap in the brilliant sunlight.

And Carla felt relief sweep over her as he stepped around to the side of the building.

6

Dan walked through the gravel lot toward the shade, wiping the sweat off his face with the tail of his shirt. He couldn't believe Carla had actually come up with a good idea. Brian Hamby seemed like a reasonable nice fellow, and if he really was good at fixing cars, Dan could sure use him.

He stepped up to the hose at the back of the store. He wanted to get most of the grime off him before Carla fixed dinner and he didn't want to hear her bitch about his leaving grease all over the bathroom sink. He reached for the faucet and stopped. The end of the hose was completely dry. He picked it up and stuck his finger up into it, then shook it. Nothing. He knelt and felt along the grassy earth underneath the hose. Dry.

He turned on the faucet and rinsed off his arms, watching the dirty water cascade down his hands to the ground. Carla hadn't used this hose all day. The bitch had lied to him. But why? If she had washed her hair upstairs, why hadn't she just said so? Why had she lied? He ought to go slap her across the room, he thought. He coiled the hose back up. Then he would see if the bitch told any more tales.

But he decided not to say anything. He was tired of finding little things she had already done. Now he wanted to just watch and wait. He wanted to catch her in the middle of something, and he knew that if he waited long enough, sooner or later he would.

And then all hell was going to break loose.

7

Brian untied him around noon.

Shane ran to the bathroom. His bladder was so full and hurting he thought he would start crying when he was finally urinating. It seemed forever before he was finished, and when he turned around, Brian was there as usual, watching him with those narrow black eyes, and Shane felt a chill pass along his spine.

In the kitchen, he fixed a peanut-butter sandwich and a glass of milk and leaned against the counter. As he ate, he stared out the window at the green hills that surrounded the house, that seemed to stretch into infinity, and he wondered if there were any houses among them he could run to, if anyone lived up there, and if they did, whether they would take him in and hide him from Brian. But even with the sun pounding down and the drowsy hum of the insects all around, the hills looked cold. Colder than the chill he had felt in the bathroom.

"I want to talk to you," Brian said behind him.

Shane didn't move.

"Look at me."

Shane did, swallowing a bit of the sandwich that didn't seem to want to go down.

Brian leaned against the wall across from him, looking down at him. "I'm sorry if I hurt you last night. I really am."

Shane took another bite and shrugged.

"I know you're mad at me, and I don't blame you a bit," Brian went on. "But I'm apologizing because I want to show you that if you're nice to me, I'll be nice to you. I promise I won't hurt you if you'll promise not to pull another stunt like that one last night. Okay?"

Shane looked down at the floor and nodded.

"Great."

There was a knock on the door, and for a second Shane thought, *It's Mom and the police and they're gonna take me home take me home take me home and I'll never have to see this place again or have to be with Brian ever again. . .* But it was only Dan Turner in his greasy clothes, with his greasy hair and greasy, humorless grin.

"Hey, Dan," Brian called, and Shane noticed him stiffen and his face turn red. "Come on in."

The yellow-haired man opened the screen door and stepped into the kitchen. "Hi." He glanced at Shane. "How you, Rob?"

"Fine."

"Good, good," he said, turning back to Brian. "Listen, Carla told me you're pretty good with cars, and I was wonderin' if you'd like to come work for me. I been swamped with work here the last couple weeks."

"Hey, great," Brian said, nodding. "I need a job really bad."

"Well, I can't pay you that much, I mean, business ain't that good." The two men laughed.

"How much can you gimme?"

Dan scratched his head under his red cap. "Well, right now. . . I could give you maybe sixty, sixty-five a week. Depends on how many people come in." He nodded toward Shane. "Your boy can come stay at the store with Carla," he said. "Keep 'em both out of trouble."

Brian nodded. "Sounds fine. Thanks a lot. I really appreciate it." He put out his hand and Dan took it, shaking it. "When you want me to start?"

Dan put his hands in his pockets. "What about tomorrow?"

"Fine with me."

"Well, I gotta get back on up to the store, see what kinda mess that wife of mine's in now," Dan said, going out the door.

"Okay. Take care."

Shane looked at Brian and saw the strangest look come across his face, something almost between relief and guilt. And suddenly it was gone, and Brian was smiling at him. "Looks like I got me a job," he said.

Shane nodded.

"At least we can get out of the house now – won't have to watch them damned soap operas all day," Brian said, and Shane could tell he was pleased. "Let's celebrate."

Brian pulled a beer out of the refrigerator and popped the top on the can. "Let's sit out on the steps."

And as they sat on the concrete blocks that were fashioned into a stoop, Shane stared out at the blue-green Kentucky hills.

They looked colder than ever.

Chapter 6

1

The next morning, Friday, was cool and rainy. It had been one week since Brian had broken into the Robinson house, and they had heard nothing of it on the news. For the first time since it had all begun, he started to breathe a little easier.

He was almost certain Dan didn't suspect anything about yesterday, about him and Carla. There had been only one horrifying moment – when Dan had come by the house to ask him about the job. Brian was sure he had found out and was coming to confront him. But today, Dan had barely cast an interested eye toward him. *He doesn't know*, Brian told himself. But there was no way he could be totally sure.

Because the rain had boxed all of them together in the store, Brian didn't have a chance to talk with Carla until almost noon, when a customer drove in, complaining about a noise coming from beneath her car. Brian had been lying beneath the old station wagon on the crawler, looking at the muffler, when he saw Carla's tennis shoes step into view beside the car. He slid himself out and looked at her. Carla smiled at him. "How's it comin'?"

"Okay. Robby keeping you on your toes?"

"Oh, yeah," she laughed. "He's a nice kid."

"Good. Oh, I meant to tell you. . . " Brian began, making up everything as he talked and lowering his voice, "I'd appreciate it if you kept a real close eye on him, you know, not let him get out of sight. We had some problems with him trying to run away before."

Carla suddenly looked concerned. "Really?"

"Yeah, so if you don't care, don't let him go outside by himself."

"No, no, of course not."

Brian looked past Carla and saw Dan's face looming white and ghostly, peering at them through the doorway the store. "Does – does he know anything about – yesterday?" he whispered.

"No. And he won't."

She turned and made her way back up the steps into the store. "He's gettin' along good," she said to the waiting customer.

Brian took one more glance at Dan and slid back under the station wagon.

2

It was the first time it had rained since Shane had been away from home, and it was a welcome change from the heat of the past few days. The only thing was, of course, that he couldn't go outside; he and Brian were stuck in the store with the man and woman.

So he sat perched atop a stack of milk crates by the window and stared out at the dismal, colorless day, waiting for Brian to finish with the lady's car so they could eat lunch.

The lady who had brought in the old station wagon sat anxiously on the bench by the garage door, sipping a Tab and chatting with Carla. Her name was Betty James, and she was on her way into Macon City when a grinding sound erupted beneath the car. "I wish he'd hurry up," she said. "I wanna know it I'm gonna need a new muffler or what."

"I'm sure he won't be much longer," Carla said.

But Shane was barely listening. He was thinking – fantasizing – about running out the door and jumping into Betty James's car just as she was driving off, about telling her everything – "He ties me up when I sleep, and he makes me take a bath in front of him!" – but he knew he would never be able to. They would stop him. Brian would grab him and pull him down outside just like he had done Wednesday night at the house, and then Shane would be dragged back into the store and told to sit still while the Turners watched over him, and then Brian would take him back to the house and beat him again. There was nothing he could do.

* * *

The afternoon was better.

Brian and Dan rode into Macon City to pick up some automobile parts, and Shane stayed with Carla. She gave him a Moonpie and a Coke and sat with him at the counter while he ate.

"So you and your dad are travelin', huh?"

"Yeah." He had no idea what Brian had told her, but he thought he had better go along with whatever she said. He wanted more than anything to tell her the truth, to tell her his real name and what had happened. Maybe she would call the police. Maybe this whole ordeal could be over. But he knew she would tell Brian, and then he would really be in trouble.

"He told me y'all're from Indiana. What town?"

"Cranston," he said without thinking. He realized what he had said and felt a light sweat break out on his face.

"Hm. You like it down here?" she went on, and Shane was grateful that she hadn't picked up on the city's name.

"Yeah, it's all right."

"Pretty borin', though, huh?"

"Yeah."

She smiled sympathetically. "I know how it is. I remember when – " The phone rang suddenly, interrupting her. She sighed and picked it up. "Turner's. . . Oh, hi, Buddy. What can I do for ya?"

Shane went back to his Moonpie, half-listening to Carla on the phone: someone named Buddy was having trouble with his tractor. Carla told him that Dan and Brian were gone and would be back in a few minutes, and then she would send one of them out there. After she had hung up, she turned back to Shane. "Your dad know anything about tractors?"

"I don't know."

"Buddy Morris is havin' trouble with one of the gears on his," she said. "It's not the first time; it does it every once in awhile. He always calls over here and Dan goes and sees about it." She noticed his empty Coke bottle. "Want another Coke?"

"No, thanks."

The Bronco pulled in outside, and he and Carla fell into a tense silence.

3

Carla watched as Dan burst through the door, followed by Brian, both of them carrying several boxes. "Bring 'em on back here," Dan said, heading toward the garage.

"Buddy Morris called," Carla said to them. "That gear on his tractor's stickin' again."

"Shit," Dan replied. He looked at Brian. "Know much about tractors?"

"Afraid not," Brian said. "Never was around 'em much."

Carla could feel Dan's hot eyes on her even though she was looking down at the counter. She turned and met his gaze. His eyes were narrow and cold.

She broke the stare, looking toward the window to the outside, and Dad said, "Well, I guess I'll go look at it." He looked at the two of them once more and then at Robby, and then he left.

"You and Robby have a good talk?" Brian asked, walking toward the front of the store.

"Yeah," she replied, watching the silver Ford pull out onto the road. She turned to the two behind her. "Wish it would do somethin' besides rain," she said, faking a smile.

"Me, too," said Brian, suddenly standing in front of her.

Carla looked up at him and saw that look in his eyes – the look she had seen yesterday, and she realized that that warmth inside her was back and stronger than ever. She licked her lips and glanced at Robby. "You wanna go upstairs and watch TV, Rob?"

"Sure," said the boy, getting up.

"The door's open up there – just go on in."

"Okay."

Neither she nor Brian moved until the sounds of the television floated down to them. And then he had her in his arms again, she was clinging to him harder than she had the first time they had made love. "Let's go to the back," she whispered hoarsely, moving to lock the door and turn off the lights.

In the dark corner under the stairs, she freed him and tasted him and his moans excited her. Then she drew his face toward her warmth, and she shivered as his hot tongue found her. And then she was pinned against the wall and he was against her, his body trembling with anticipation and effort. The smell of him – a mixture of sweat and outdoors and smoke – seemed to stir up something new in her; her hands found the warm flesh of his back beneath his shirt, and she held onto it, pulling him against her. They tore at each other's clothes, taking off only what was necessary. And then he was inside her, pushing and pushing and she wanted to wrap herself around him and push back. And then suddenly the heated rush was over and they melted as they sank to the floor in the cool darkness, sweating and breathless.

She put her face against his chest and closed her eyes. After a while, she reached up and stroked his cheek. "What time is it?"

Brian glanced at his watch. "Nearly five."

"Oh, no!" Carla jumped up and fumbled with her clothes, pulling up her jeans and smoothing down her t-shirt. "Dan's been gone almost an hour. He could be back any minute."

Behind her, Brian had buckled his belt and was pulling his cap down on his head. "We'll go on home, I guess." He kissed her on the mouth and looked into her eyes for an eternity, then stepped around to the foot of the stairs. "Rob? Let's go."

The boy came slowly down the stairs. "Thanks for lettin' me watch TV," he told Carla.

"You're welcome," she said, smiling.

The truck pulled in outside, and they heard the slam of the door and Dan's slow, crunching steps as he made his way toward the store. "I see you already closed up," he said to Carla as he came inside with the key, slipping out of his jacket.

"Yeah," she said. "We hadn't had any customers since before you left, so I just went on ahead and locked up."

"Good night," Brian said as he and Robby started toward the door.

"Okay," Dan replied. "See y'all tomorrow."

"'Night," Carla called as she locked the screen door behind them. She pulled the heavy door closed and locked it just as Brian and Robby drove off in their blue pickup. Outside, the shadows were long in the orange light of the late afternoon sun as it finally broke through the rainclouds, and she was glad to see it. "Sun's out," she said to Dan. She turned and he was looking at her coldly, and she thought *devil in his eyes oh God the devil's in his eyes*. "What's wrong?" she said. He took a step toward her. "What do you want for dinner?" His rough hands grabbed her wrists and he jerked her around to look at him. "You're hurtin' me," she said, and her mouth was dry as sand.

"You bitch," he hissed. "You think I can't smell it on ya?"

"What?" Her knees became rubber, and she fell against the doorframe.

He grabbed her face and jerked it up, forcing her to look into his eyes. "You fucked him, didn't ya?"

She said nothing, trying to look away.

"Didn't ya?" He turned around and pushed the cash register off the counter. It exploded on the concrete floor with the ringing of the bell and the scattering of change. Dan turned back to her and grabbed her shoulders, shaking and shaking her until her vision went fuzzy. "You fuckin' whore!" he spat. "Goddamn you! Goddamn you!" He slapped her and grinned horribly as she cried out. He hit her again, this time with his fist. Through the blinding red pain, she heard him say, "Bitch. I'll teach you to fuck everything that comes through the door. What'd you do with his boy, let him watch?" He stooped and peered into her face. "I hope it was good."

She looked up and stared at him for what seemed a long time. "Oh, it was," she said finally. He blinked, and she could tell she had shocked him. "Better than you'll ever be." She looked him up and down. "And you should see his body. So strong. Not fat and white and hairless like you. And that pitiful little thing between your legs you call – "

He hit her then – a full blow to the face, cutting her brow with his ring. He grabbed her arms and pulled her up the stairs. "No!" she screamed, but it was as though he couldn't hear her. She tried kicking him, but it was impossible to reach him on the steps.

Upstairs, he shoved her down onto the bed, and she could taste the blood from where she had bitten her lip. "I'll teach ya," she heard him say. "I'll show you who's a man around here."

Being on top of her like this must have excited him somehow, having her pinned below him, her body rising and falling with her breath. He grabbed hold of the collar of her shirt and ripped it down the front. Her breasts lolled out of the cloth. "Oh, so you are a whore. Whores never wear bras."

"Stop it," she breathed. "Please."

He slapped her again and jerked her jeans and panties down her hips. "I'll teach ya," he muttered again. She heard the sound of his fly unzipping, and through bleary eyes saw him spit into his hand and rub the saliva along the length of his hardness. He crammed himself into her, and she cried out with the pain. When he was finished, he stood and rebuckled his jeans as she lay crying and bleeding and tangled in the sheets. "I'll be back," he told her. "And then I'll take care of all of it." He stormed out the door and down the stairs, and in a moment she heard the Bronco roar to life. And he was gone.

She dragged herself out of bed and sank to her knees on the floor. Reaching into a drawer, she pulled out a clean T-shirt. The pulse of hot pain in her head was sickening; she pulled the remnants of cloth off her shoulders and doubled over, vomiting on the rug. She wiped her mouth on the bedsheet and crawled into the shirt.

She had to get to Brian. What if Dan stormed down there and killed him and Robby? But thankfully she had heard him drive off in the other direction – toward town. She had to get to the house as quickly as possible.

She inched her way downstairs, careful not to slip and tumble to the bottom, and outside to the calm of the late afternoon.

She stumbled in the direction of the house, not really seeing where she was going. It seemed to take forever, traveling along the side of the road through the high weeds and muddy ditch. But as she reached the yard, she dropped to her hands and knees and crawled toward the farmhouse, too weak to walk the last few steps. She sank to the concrete stoop and banged her fist against the black frame of the screen door. Blood had run into her eyes from the cut on her brow, and she could barely see for the sting.

The door creaked open, and she heard Brian's voice: "My God! Carla! What happened?" He was beside her at once. She was vaguely aware that Robby was behind them, watching. "How bad are you hurt?"

"He knows, Brian."

She felt him stiffen. "What?"

"He knows. . . "

"*He* did this to you?"

She nodded faintly and swallowed, tasting the iron tang of blood.

"That son of a bitch," he muttered. "Help me get her in the house," he said to the boy.

She felt the arms lifting, helping her stagger through the kitchen into the living room. She sat on the sofa and fell back, seemed to fall forever, and floated on the feathery softness until something cold and damp touched her face. She opened her eyes to find Brian sponging her forehead with a washcloth. "Son of a bitch," he said again, mopping the blood. "Get another rag," he told Robby, and as the boy left, Carla saw something gleam in Brian's eyes – the same gleam she had seen in Dan's eyes when he had punched her. "That's not all," she managed to say as the boy returned and handed Brian another washcloth.

"What?" Brian asked, not moving. But Carla couldn't speak, couldn't tell him. He shook her. "Carla! What else did he do to you?"

It was forever before she was able to answer: "He raped me, Brian," she said, feeling the flood of tears pour out. He was holding her, rocking her as she sobbed. She grasped him tightly, her sobs a mixture of relief and guilt.

"Bastard," Brian spat.

"Please," she begged. She drew away from him and looked right into his eyes. "He's gone away for now, but he's comin' back. Please, Brian. Help me. He'll kill us all."

4

Brian pulled a bottle of Jack Daniel's out from a cabinet in the kitchen and brought back in to her. "Drink some of this." She turned it up and grimaced at the taste. She handed it back to him and wiped her mouth with her hand. "Better?"

She nodded. "A little." She sat up in the bed. "Please. Please," she begged. "We've got to do something. He's comin' back, and when he does, he's gonna kill us."

Brian looked at her with pity, rage and terror. "Let's just leave. We can take off right now."

She was shaking her head. "He'd come after us. You don't know him, Brian. He wouldn't stop 'til he got us."

Brian rubbed his eyes. She was talking out of her head, he thought. "Why don't you just call the police?"

"Yeah. Right. What do I tell them? 'I think my husband might be gonna kill me'?"

"You tell them he raped you."

She looked down. "Around here they don't call it rape if the guy's your husband."

"What about beating you up?"

She looked down at her clenched hands. Silent tears slipped down her cheeks and splashed on her t-shirt. "You know how many times I've made that call? How many times the sheriff's come out here? How many times he's told 'em I fell down the stairs and hit my head and didn't know what I was talkin' about? And then when they've all slapped each other on the back and had a good laugh about Dan's clumsy wife, he's come back in and beat me twice as bad." She glanced back at Brian and her eyes were red and glassy. "You don't understand how bad this is," she said. "He's gonna kill all of us – even Robby – if we don't kill him first."

Brian's heart stopped. "Kill him first? Jesus Christ, do you know what you're saying?"

"Yes," she said.

"Do you?" There was a fire burning deep in Brian's gut. "No. I don't want to get mixed up in this."

"I can't do it by myself," she sobbed.

"Then don't do it!" He turned away. "Let's just get our stuff and leave." he said. "We'll pack up some clothes and head out right now."

"He'll follow us!" she screamed. "He'll just find us and kill us somewhere else."

He stared at her. "Are you fucking crazy? If Dan can find us, don't you think the police can find us?"

She wiped her forehead with one of the damp cloths and looked at the blood on it. "We've got to do it. We don't have a choice."

"*I've* got a choice," Brian said, jumping up. "I'm not getting involved in this."

"You're already involved," Carla said, and he knew it was true.

He sat back down on the bed. He rubbed his temples, trying to quell the dull throb. "I don't know what to do," he said finally. "I can't do this. You don't understand. I *can't*. I'm not getting involved in another death."

Carla looked at him with her red eyes. "What?"

"Look," Brian said, "it's all gonna come out sooner or later anyway, so it might as well be now."

"What are you talkin' about?" Carla asked.

Brian blew out a breath and looked at her. "First of all, my name's not Brian Hamby, it's Brian DeCanto." He motioned toward the boy. "He isn't my son, either. His real name's Shane Robinson. I accidentally shot his dad."

Carla was staring at him. "You. . . killed him?"

Brian nodded. "It was an accident, I swear to God." He told her everything – all about picking up the dead cat, going into the house, finding the gun and the struggle with Robinson. And when he was finished, the inside of his mouth tasted like something caught in the drain of the kitchen sink.

Carla looked down at the bloody cloth in her hand. "So then you had to take his son because he saw what happened."

"Right. I put him in my truck and we started driving – I didn't care where we wound up, but I sure as hell wanted to get away from there. And that's how we ended up here." He let out a breath, one that he seemed to have been holding since the whole ordeal had begun.

"What about his mother?" Carla asked.

"Probably looking for us right now."

Carla looked awed. "My God," she whispered.

Brian stood up. "Come on."

Carla looked at him. "What're we gonna do?"

"I'm packing up our stuff and we're leaving. If you want to go with us we can swing by your place and you can throw a few things together." Brian gently took her face in his hand. "I'm sorry. I'm not doing anything else."

5

After Brian and Shane had packed their few belongings, they all piled into Brian's truck and headed up to the store. Dan was nowhere to be seen.

Carla led them upstairs to the tiny apartment and pulled a worn dusty suitcase from beneath the bed, then began pulling clothes from the dresser and shoving them in it. She wasn't sure what all she would need. In the end she piled in all the clothes she could and all the money she could find in the place. It wasn't much – a little over three hundred dollars – but it was a start.

There was around four thousand in the bank, though, and that was where part two of the plan began. Tonight they would stay in a motel in Macon City, and in the morning Carla would go into the bank and draw out most of the money. It was risky to stay in town tonight, but they needed the cash too badly to not take the chance.

She latched the suitcase and looked around the sparse room. "That's it, I guess." Brian took the suitcase from her and they made their way down the stairs and through the store. They stepped through the screen door out onto the porch. It was almost dark now. The red sun had already sunk below the misty hills, leaving a purple glow in the sky.

Carla felt a sudden burst of panic as she heard the faint, distant rumble of a heavy vehicle grow louder. She tried to take a deep breath, but it caught inside her. Headlights popped into view, and Carla saw red with each thump of her heart. Even in the dim light, she could descry the dent in the side of the silver Bronco – the result of an accident Dan had had in town. "Oh, my God," she said. "It's him."

Brian put a hand on her shoulder. "You take the suitcase. I'll handle this."

She swung the suitcase into the bed of Brian's truck and stood still as stone as the Bronco pulled into the lot. The door swung open and Dan climbed out. He stood there, looking at all three of them. "Figured I'd find you all here," he said, and Carla could tell he was drunk.

Brian stepped up. "Dan, we don't want any trouble. Just let us leave."

Dan moved toward him. "Well, you got trouble. You think you can just sweep in here, fuck my wife and leave? You think I can just let you do that?"

Brian backed up a step. "I'm sorry, Dan. It wasn't like that."

Dan had reached the front of the Bronco. "I gave you a job. Let you and your boy move into the house. And you just go and screw me over like that."

Carla saw something gleaming in Dan's hand, and she realized he was holding a tire iron. Brian saw it, too. His eyes grew wide. "Put it down, Dan," he said. "Let's talk this out."

Dan continued to move forward. "I ain't talkin' shit."

Brian was now pinned against the porch. "Back off, Dan."

The boy had moved closer to Carla. His eyes were round and frightened.

That was when she saw the rusted pipe lying at the edge of the lot, just barely visible in the weeds. Slowly she knelt and grabbed it. It was heavy in her hand. She raised it above her head and stepped toward Dan.

6

Brian could feel the concrete porch pressing into his back. Dan was still coming at him with the tire iron. If only he had the gun. He could hold Dan off while Shane and Carla got in the truck. But it was packed away in his bag.

That was when he saw Carla behind Dan. Coming toward them with something in her hand – a pipe. He looked back at Dan. He was still moving toward him with the tire iron.

Suddenly, Shane was screaming from the side of the truck. "Look out! Look out!"

Dan swung around toward the voice. "What?"

Carla swung the pipe as hard as she could and it connected with the back of Dan's head. The sound was sickening. But worse was the look on Dan Turner's face – every muscle contorted in pain, his skin waxy and colorless. He fell into the gravel with a crunch.

Behind him, Carla stood like a statue, the pipe still raised in the air. She sobbed suddenly, her bugging eyes not moving from the man's body. "Is he dead?" she cried, her voice trembling and cracking.

Brian stared at her. "What the fuck, Carla? What the *fuck*?" He grabbed hold of Dan's arm and turned the man over. Dan had fallen on his face, and his nose and mouth were covered with blood. Brian stuck an ear to the man's chest and heard nothing. "I think he's dead. I think you killed him."

Carla dropped the pipe with a clang. "I killed him. I really killed him."

Brian put a hand on her shoulder and nudged her toward the truck. "We've got to get out of here."

Carla looked at him, panicked. "We can't leave him like this. Somebody will see him."

He looked around. "We'll move him then. We'll put him inside the store."

It was not an easy task. Dan was a huge man, and the dead weight was more than Brian could manage alone. He took Dan's arms, and with Shane and Carla at the man's feet, they managed to move him up on the porch and slide him inside the door to the store. He took Carla's keys and locked up. "No one will find him for a while," he said, "at least not before we're gone in the morning."

They piled into the cab of the Ford. Carla was screaming and sobbing and babbling and Shane was crying as well. "Shut up!" Brian yelled at Carla. He leaned over Shane and slapped her hard. She glared at him, suddenly quieting. "It's over!" he told her. "Just shut the fuck up and keep quiet – both of you – 'til we get to town." He pulled the truck onto the highway and they headed south for Macon City.

Chapter 7

1

The woman was still whimpering when they entered the motel room a few minutes later. Shane watched her in the corner of his eye; the sight of her gave him a strange feeling, a mixture of pity and revulsion. A warmth spread across his cheeks to his ears, and he realized his face was turning red.

"Sit down in that chair there, Shane," Brian told him.

Shane did, watching silently as Carla moved to the bed in front of him.

"I can't believe it," Carla whispered. It was the first thing she had said since they had left the store. "He's dead. It's all over." She looked at Brian, her eyes puffy and red. "It's all over."

Brian paced back and forth. "What the fuck were you thinking?" he spat at her. "I told you I wasn't getting involved in killing him."

"I'm sorry," she said. "I thought he was gonna hurt you." Her tears started anew, spilling down her cheeks in rivulets. "I was trying to help."

Brian whirled around at her. "Help! You *killed* him, Carla!" He flopped down on the other bed and blew out a breath. "You have really fucked everything up, you know that?"

Carla put up her hands. "Don't do this, Brian, don't do this now."

"I ought to just leave your ass here." He nodded at Shane. "And you, too. I ought to just get in my truck and start driving and leave both of you."

Carla gave a loud cry. "No. . . you can't leave me, Brian, you *can't.*"

"Like hell. We had a deal. We were just gonna pack up and go. You're the one that changed everything by bashing his goddamned head in."

Carla had drawn herself up on the bed and was curled around a pillow. "Stop," she said, and her voice was just barely a whisper. "Please stop." She buried her face in the pillow and sobbed.

Brian stomped around the room and ran his fingers through his hair. He settled down on the bed beside Carla and pulled her close. "Stop it, now, stop it." She turned toward him and cried into his shoulder. "I'm sorry," he said. "Everything will work out all right. Tomorrow morning we'll go to the bank and then we'll be off. Heading south."

"But what if somebody finds him before we can get the money out? What if they know at the bank? What if – "

Brian shushed her by putting his fingers over her lips. "Stop worrying'." He looked toward Shane. "Right now I think we all just need some sleep."

* * *

The two double beds were old, nasty things that looked as though they had been salvaged from a condemned hospital. Shane's limbs had been tied to the convenient metal frames at the foot and head of his bed, and he knew it would be hard to sleep in such a position. To top everything off, there was a rattling squeak deep within the springs that seemed to grind with his slightest movement. At least the place was cool, and he was grateful for the hum of the air conditioner beneath the window.

Tears suddenly stung his eyes, flowing down to wet his pillow in the darkness. He was trapped – more alone and frightened than he had ever been in his life. And something seemed to wash over him – a sort of understanding. For the first time he knew the meaning of being cornered, ensnared. For the first time since the mouse.

Oh, God, the mouse. That had happened a little over a year ago, but he could remember it vividly.

He had been at the mall with his mother and Tommy Ray, and while his mom had gone off to browse the clothing stores, he and Tommy had escaped into Video Game World for awhile. But soon Tommy was bored with Tron and Dragon's Lair and Star Castle. "I know somethin' neat we can do," he told Shane. "Let's go to the pet store."

"What for?"

Tommy showed him two quarters in his hand. "Got fifty more cents?"

Five minutes later, as they stood before the counter of Pets, Inc., Shane realized with giddy apprehension what was going to happen. The crudely-lettered sign read:

You may feed our Python

$1.00

Your Treat

He watched the four quarters spin like tops as Tommy tossed them onto the counter. "We wanna feed the snake," Tommy announced to the pudgy, bespectacled man behind the register.

"You in here again?" the clerk asked, his eyebrows going up. "Long as you keep coming in I won't ever have to feed that python again."

Tommy laughed and glanced over at Shane as the man rang up the sale. "What's wrong with you, Shane?" he asked.

"What're you gonna do?"

"Come on," Tommy said, leading him toward the back of the store. "It's neat."

Shane followed him somewhat hesitantly. He had never liked snakes anyway, and the thought of maybe touching one nearly put him into a frenzy. "Tommy, I – "

"What is wrong with you, man?"

"I – I don't wanna touch a snake," he blurted, embarrassed.

Tommy laughed. "We don't have to touch it or anything. We just pay for the mouse."

Shane shot him an alarming look. "Mouse?"

Tome gave him his you-have-the-IQ-of-a-lightbulb look. "Yes, stupid. That's what snakes eat. This snake, anyways."

Shane suddenly felt relieved. Looking at a dead mouse wouldn't be so bad.

But a moment later when the clerk dropped the trembling, quaking, very-much-alive albino mouse into the python's glass tank, he felt the panic numb him.

The mouse appeared disoriented for a few seconds, but then it began frantically pawing at the slick glass sides of the cage. Shane watched, frozen. The mouse's panicky, wide pink eyes searched for a quick escape while its quivering nose sniffed at the danger it knew was so close. Behind the small creature, the python began its slow, lazy movements toward the scurrying in the corner of its tank.

"Make it stop, Tommy," Shane whispered, his eyes never moving.

Beside him, Tommy said, "What's wrong with you? You chicken-shit or somethin'?"

Shane watched, sickened yet fascinated, as the snake suddenly struck at the white mouse, stunning it. Instantly, the mouse was still, its glassy eyes unseeing. A dark spot of red blood began to seep through its fine white fur. Almost grotesquely beautiful, the python slowly wrapped itself around its prey and squeezed until the fluttery breath of the rodent had been stilled. The snake unhinged its jaw and began to push the whole body of the mouse inside its open, vile mouth. That was when Shane turned and bolted.

Then in the restroom while he wiped the rest of the vomit off his mouth and spat into the commode,

Tommy said behind him, "You have got to be the biggest chicken-shit I know."

Shane stared into the toilet. He avoided Tommy's eyes because of what he had seen while the mouse was going eaten. Tommy had been enthralled, enraptured. *Excited.*

He glanced at Tommy only briefly. "You suck," he told him. "You suck fags." It had been the worst thing he could think of right then.

* * *

And now tears flowed freely. He was crying for everything, for nothing. He was crying for the mouse and the wild, desperate look in its eyes. He was crying for his father. He was crying for his mother. He was crying for Bowser. He was crying for the man lying dead up the road miles away, the man he had seen killed. Slowly, eventually, he cried himself to sleep.

2

Carla knew it was nervousness about tomorrow keeping her awake. That and the quiet hum of the air conditioner that seemed to put out warm air. The boy was tossing on his squeaky bed, too; every time Carla began to drift off, a creak from the springs brought her fully awake where she lay in the crook of Brian's arm.

She ran her fingertips across his chest – warm and solid and crisp with the bristle of hair. She put her thigh across his hips and felt herself grow warm and wet. If the boy had not been in the room she would have touched herself, even as Brian slept beside her. But there would be more opportunities. She turned over and tried to force her mind to go blank. There would be many chances to make love.

But if he left her, if she awoke in the morning to find him gone, she had no idea what she would do. Her life would be over. There would be nothing left for her – no hope, no future. She might as well be dead.

3

The bitch had tried to kill him.

And now, even as the large knot on his head began to pound again with the excruciating pain, he thought of all the things he would do to her if he ever saw her again. He would kill her. Oh, yes. But he would fuck her first.

When he had first woke up, dusty and groggy on the concrete floor, he felt as though he were coming down from a three-day drunk. His hands had instinctively gone to his head, and he felt lump the size of a baseball. He vaguely remembered Hamby's boy screaming, "Look out! Look out!" He remembered turning toward the sound. And Carla swinging something right into the base of his skull. . . And when he was awake enough to sit up and look around, he could see he was completely alone in the quiet of the store.

His nose was bleeding. The blood splashed hot and dirty onto the floor with sickening finality. For some reason, he had never before thought about the floor being concrete. But then he had never had his face this close to it, either. He touched his face and felt his nose give a little with gritty fluidity, as if it were filled with a mixture of sand and water. He leaned sideways and vomited.

He leaned back against the counter and shook his head, trying to clear it. It was still dark, and a glance at his watch told him it was almost four in the morning. Shit. There was no telling where they were by now.

Slowly – very slowly – he stood. But his head swam, and he squatted back down. He would have to take it slowly. He saw the cash register still lay on its side from this afternoon, looking like some prehistoric cyborg that had been shot down and now spilled its blood of metal coins across the floor. With everything he had in him, he managed to pull himself to his feet and reach for the telephone. And then he stopped.

He could call the sheriff and have him chase them down and bring them back. But then Carla would spill it all about how he had beat her up and, yes, how he had raped her. And besides, whatever they did to her could never, never punish her like what he could do to her. He hung up the phone and crawled upstairs, leaving a trail of blood droplets.

In the darkness, his hands groped for the whiskey bottle and found it. He raised it to his lips and drank it down, sharp and biting and good. The he made his way to the toilet and pulled on the blinding, piercing light. He felt the lump again while waiting for his eyes to adjust. Goddamn! The thought of a concussion passed his mind, but he shrugged it off; the dizziness had passed and now he could stand. He would be all right. He took a wet washcloth from the towel rack and wiped gingerly at his nose. It was probably broken, but he could breathe and that was enough. He sure as hell didn't want to go to the emergency room and answer a bunch of damn questions. The blood was coming off, and even though his nose was swollen and blue, he knew he would be all right. He turned out the light and stumbled back toward the bottle by the television.

He picked up the Jack Daniel's and felt its heaviness. Good – it was practically full. He flipped on the TV and fell back into his recliner. The farm report was already on, and the announcer looked like some pansy that had never been in a barn in his life. "Faggot," he whispered. He took another swallow of the whiskey.

4

The daylight seemed to have turned against her, Carla thought as she stepped out of Brian's truck into the bright sunlight. There seemed to be something evil about the sun; perhaps it was that the light showed her to be a frail, frightened woman. But she lifted her head confidently. They must not know she was afraid. Some people could smell fear – like dogs. And with that thought in her head, she stepped through the double doors of the Macon City Farmers Bank and Trust and made her way to the nearest window. The bank was nearly deserted this early on a Saturday and she was grateful. She saw no one she knew.

The teller was young, about twenty, and her reddish-brown hair was cut in a very flattering fashion, a style Carla at once liked and marked as how she would like her own to be. "Good morning. Can I help you?"

"Yes," Carla said, setting her purse on the counter. "I need to make a withdrawal." She pulled out her checkbook. "I'm not sure how much is in there, though."

The girl took a piece of paper and began copying something off the checks. "I'll need your account number. Just a minute. I'll look up your balance on the microfiche." She disappeared into the back of the bank.

Carla's heart began to pound. She was going back there to call the police. She was going to tell them the crazy Turner woman who killed her husband last night was here trying to draw out all his money. And when the teller suddenly stepped back into the window, Carla's heart almost stopped. "Mrs. Turner?"

"Yes?"

"You have four thousand, one fifty-two and sixty cents."

"Okay." She began making out a check. "I'm going to need four thousand."

"I'll just need some ID please."

Carla reached over to dig out her driver's license.

"Would you like large bills?" the girl asked.

Carla laughed.

5

In the truck, Shane sat between Brian and the woman, staring out the window until his eyes were dry and stinging, then blinking and doing it again. His fast-food breakfast was heavy in his stomach, and he caught himself dozing several times, the drowsiness coming and going like waves washing over him and then heading back out to sea.

He had lost count of the days he and Brian had been together. It seemed like a month, though he was sure it had been no more than a week. Sometimes the desire to go him hit him so hard and so fast that he thought he would vomit. He would feel the rage swell up in him, strong and explosive, only to be released in a silent flow of tears.

The thought of being with his mother again was all he lived for. But now, as they drove farther south, even that hope seemed to be dimming. And there wasn't one thing he could do about it.

So he sat back in the cab of the truck as the warm wind played over him, and he watched the countryside roll by.

* * *

About forty-five minutes after they had left Macon City, they entered the dirty, squalid little town of Wellsboro, which, Carla informed them, lay on the Kentucky-Tennessee border. Minutes later, the blue Ford truck whizzed across the Tennessee state line, and Carla and Brian gave shouts of joy. Brian leaned over and kissed Carla on the cheek, saying something Shane didn't hear.

The radio was playing Ricky Nelson's "Travelin' Man," and there was a cry of delight from Carla and Brian as they began to sing along.

Between them, Shane watched out the window and felt tears sliding down his cheeks.

6

When Dan woke up, the sun was streaming through the windows, and a big burly reporter was interviewing a real cute blonde girl. She was saying something about marketing research. But Dan was looking at her tits. Big ones. They pushed up against her blouse like two globes.

He stood and made his way into the bathroom. His nose was like concrete and he could barely breathe. He blew it and a thick membrane of bloody mucus came out with a sharp pain. But at least he could breathe again.

It was after his shower, while he was drying off, that the local news came on. Still naked, he stepped back toward the TV so he could watch it. And that was when a picture of Brian Hamby's boy flashed across the screen: Shane Robinson. . . missing for a week. . . father found dead. . . probably a burglar. . .

Dan sat down. Stunned. Robby Hamby was this Robinson kid. He couldn't believe it. But the photograph was there, almost accusing. And then the boy's mother was on, Liz Robinson, sobbing and pleading and beautiful, and Dan felt something give in his chest a little. He flipped off the TV and stood.

Mitchell Robinson. That was the name they had given on the report. He made his way downstairs to the phone. He still hadn't dressed, but he didn't care. He got the number from long-distance information and dialed it, his heart quickening. It rang once. Twice. Three times. And then a voice, barely audible, said, "Yes?"

For a moment he wanted to hang up, to just leave it all alone and get on with his life. But then he thought of the woman's pleading, desperate face on his television and the bastard that had taken his wife and the boy, and he said, "Liz Robinson?"

"Yes?"

"This is Dan Turner in Macon City, Kentucky. I know somethin' about your son."

Chapter 8

1

Late in the afternoon, Brian pulled onto a dirt road just off the main highway and followed it for about a mile or so until they came to a small, sparsely overgrown clearing. "We might as well spend the night here and decide where we want to go in the mornin'."

"But this looks like somebody's farm," Carla said. "I don't know. . . "

"Don't worry," Brian told her. "Don't look like it's been used for quite a while. We can probably even have a little fire."

"That would be nice," Carla said.

Shane felt a sudden rumbling in his belly. "I'm hungry," he said. It was the first thing he had said since they had stopped for lunch at a tiny grocery that made sandwiches for a dollar.

Brian glanced at him. "There's still three or four sandwiches in the cooler, but I thought we oughta save them for supper."

Shane nodded and looked away. He would have to ignore the hunger pangs.

Brian stepped out of the truck and Carla followed him. "What kinda weeds are these big tall ones?" she asked.

"Hell if I know," Brian said. "Looks like some kinda ragweed or somethin'."

But Shane wasn't listening. He was suddenly aware that he was alone in the truck. And Brian's keys dangled from the ignition. Shane had never driven before, but he had watched his parents plenty of times, watched how carefully they pressed the accelerator, how they eased on the brakes. And his dad had even taught him how to start his mother's station wagon. He could do it. He could drive off and leave them. He pictured himself, some juvenile Indiana Jones roaring across the clearing toward Brian and Carla where they now stood talking. They would look up at the noise and be frozen in terror as Shane closed the distance between them and the pickup. And then he would flatten them. He would run over them and over them and over them until they were just black circles on the ground. And then he would head off for home.

And now, sitting on the sticky vinyl seat, he began to hum the theme to Raiders of the Lost Ark. He slowly slid across until he was behind the wheel. He could barely reach the pedals, but it would be good enough. He reached for the keys.

He jumped as Brian's hairy hand grabbed his arm. "What the fuck are you doing?"

Shane bit his lower lip. *I'm not gonna cry, not gonna cry, not gonna cry.*

But everything flew out of him as Brian gave him a hard boxy slap across his jaw and neck. "Get outa there." Brian pulled him down into the weeds and Shane fell at the man's feet.

"Brian! Stop it!" Carla screamed. "Stop it!" Then she was there, clinging to Brian's arm. "What're you doin' to him?" She knelt down by Shane and helped him up. "Are you okay, honey?"

Shane nodded, edging closer to her.

"He was gonna drive away!" Brian was screaming at Carla. "You would have just stood there. He was ready to turn the damn key for chrissake!"

Carla hugged Shane's head to her. "Leave him alone," she spat. "You're the one who left the keys in the truck in the first place."

Brian glared at her for a minute, then whirled around and pounded the hood of the truck with his fist.

"I can't really blame him for wantin' to run away, though, can you?" Carla said, her voice softer.

Brian looked around at them. "No. I guess not." He walked away a few steps. "I just don't know what we're gonna do with him. Half the time I wish he *would* run away so we don't have to fool with him. I mean, we can't keep him with us forever. We can't keep tying him up every night 'til he's eighteen for God's sake."

"Yeah," Carla whispered. "I know." She smoothed back Shane's sweaty hair. "Somethin'll work out."

* * *

It was night now.

At dusk, Brian had found some good dried branches in the woods that rimmed the clearing, and he was able to build a little campfire. They sat on a log by it now, bathed in the orange light, eating the rest of the soggy sandwiches. The tuna salad tasted awful, but Shane was too hungry to complain. Brian and Carla were looking at the map of Tennessee, trying to figure out exactly where they were, but Shane tried to ignore them. He didn't want to know because he was a long, long way from home, and if he knew how far, he would probably go crazy.

So he sat and stared into the fire. The snapping and popping and the black odor of the smoke took him back to the night last autumn when he and his father had gone fishing at the creek not far from their house.

It had been a clear night, like this one, and his dad built a big fire for them to roast hot dogs over. And after they had eaten, he poured water on it. They had brought a Coleman lantern with then, but he turned that off, too. Shane asked why, and his father told him snakes were attracted to the light. "You take a lantern out on the water at night," he said, "and the snakes'll crawl right up in the boat with you. You gotta be careful if you're gonna fish at night." And Shane shivered, thinking about the python and the white mouse. So they fished in the dark until the yellow moon rose like a ghost above the treetops.

They had only caught a couple of catfish when an eerie scream began to echo through the woods. "What's that?" Shane whispered.

"Bobcat," his father told him. "We'd better get back to the house."

And they began the long hike toward home, the Coleman lantern giving the dark woods a spooky glow.

The scream continued, each time from a different place. "Are there more of them?" Shane asked.

"No," his dad said. "It's the same one. He's circlin' us." And they hurried back to the house, both expecting the bobcat to suddenly appear in front of them. But it didn't.

And now, as Shane sat in front of the fire, he wondered if there might be bobcats in these woods. And snakes. But it didn't matter if there were. Right now he was more scared of Brian than of any bobcat.

2

Dan had been to the police that afternoon. He told them all they wanted to know. It had been so easy to lie to them. No one knew the difference. Brian Hamby, he explained, had tried to kill him and had taken Carla away along with the boy. It was simple, believable, and, luckily, not entirely a falsehood – Carla never could have pulled such a stunt by herself. She wasn't that bright.

But it had been for Shane Robinson's sake only that he had gone to the police in the first place. There was no telling what Hamby was doing to that boy, had been doing to him all along. It just made Dan sick.

And now he wheeled the silver Bronco onto the parking lot of the B & N Truckstop. He and Liz Robinson were supposed to meet here in about fifteen minutes. He didn't know why; she just said on the phone they should meet and talk about things, that maybe they could help each other.

But Dan couldn't help noticing she had picked obviously neutral ground for them to meet on – a three-hour drive for each of them – probably for her own personal safety. He understand that; he knew there were some pretty sick people out there who would just love an opportunity like this to take advantage of her when she was so fragile. But she would see he wasn't one of them.

He sat in the quiet darkness of the truck for a minute, studying the cars on the lot. There were quite a few people here for it to be so close to nine o'clock. She might be here already, but he didn't know what kind of car she drove. Not that it mattered.

He made his way inside through the sea of faded jeans, plaid shirts, and billed caps at the tables and started to take a seat at the counter. But then he saw her way in the back, her light blonde hair a bob that turned under at the shoulders. It had to be her. She was staring into a cup of coffee, looking a bit more composed than she had on television, but her blue eyes were weak and watery.

Suddenly nervous, Dan eased off his cap and smoothed down his hair, then headed for the table. "Liz Robinson?" She looked up. "I'm Dan Turner." He stuck out his hand and she stood and took it.

"Hi," she said quietly. "Good to meet you."

"Yeah," he said, sitting down across from her and hiding his cap under his leg.

"I don't suppose you've heard anything else since you talked to the police," she said.

He shook his head. "Naw. They just said they'd be gettin' right on it."

The waitress, a haggard woman with dark circles beneath her eyes, took Dan's order for coffee and brought it promptly. Liz watched him stir a packed of sugar into the cup. "You don't know how much I would love to take a gun and blow that bastard away," she said.

Dan chuckled. "You know, ma'am, I'd like to do the same thing myself."

Liz's eyes were suddenly hard. "I'd do it, too. You can't imagine how. . . horrible it was, walking in and finding Mitch like that. And then when Shane was gone I – I just went crazy."

Dan stared at his coffee. "Hm."

She put her hand on his arm and he jumped. "Do you think Shane's all right? The police are so confused. I mean, there's been no ransom note or phone call or anything."

Dan looked at her. "I don't know. I mean, every time I was around him he looked okay. I'm sure he's still. . . " He stopped. He had started to say "still alive," but he was sure that would only upset her. "He's all right," he finished.

"How are you?" she asked. "Your nose looks pretty bad."

He reached up and felt the scabs and bruises across his face. "Still hurts, but it's not that bad. I just can't breathe sometimes because of all the dried blood and stuff."

Liz nodded and looked away, fingering the collar of her blouse. "I just wish that man was dead. I'd give anything to – to. . . "

"Kill him?"

She nodded. "Yes. I'd like to splatter his blood all over the country."

Dan smiled. "I think you'd have to stand in line."

She smiled back weakly. "Even if the police catch him, there's nothing they can do to him that can justify what he did."

Dan nodded and looked away. "I know." He licked his lips. "How you holdin' up?"

She sighed. "Good, I guess. I'm tired."

"Yeah. I know what'cha mean."

She took a sip of coffee. "I just hope it's over soon."

3

Carla awoke slowly and blissfully, the morning sunlight in her eyes. In spite of all they had done, in spite of the ground being hard and cold, she had slept better last night than she had in a long time. She reached over for Brian and found him gone. With panic, she sat up in the sleeping bag and spotted him stirring the ashes from the fire a few yards away.

He turned. "Good morning. How'd you sleep?"

She smiled and brushed a strand of frizzy hair out of her eyes. "Real good." She glanced over to where Shane still lay asleep. The night before, since there were only two sleeping bags, Carla had taken one and Shane the other, leaving Brian to sleep on a blanket between them, his wrist securely bound to the boy's with a length of old clothesline. "You took the rope off him," Carla said.

"It's okay," he told her. "I'm watchin' him."

Carla smiled and stepped out of the bag. "It's Sunday."

Brian looked at her. "Yeah. So?"

Carla laughed. "Well, I was just thinkin' about my mama. She used to call me up every Sunday and beg me to go to church with her."

"You go?"

Carla shook her head. "No way."

"How come?"

She shrugged. "I don't know. I mean, I believe in God and everything, but I just didn't like church. It was too. . . too – "

"Our passenger's wakin' up."

Carla looked around just as Shane stretched. She walked over to him and knelt down. "Good mornin', honey," she said. Then she winced; there was a bruise on Shane's neck where Brian had hit him the day before.

"Let's get ready to go," Brian said.

"What time is it?" Carla asked.

"About six-thirty; I'd hate for somebody to see us in this field."

Carla helped Shane out of the sleeping bag and then began folding it. "Where are we goin', Brian?"

Brian walked over, the map in his back pocket. "I was lookin' at the map before you got up. There's a town called Oak Creek just south of Atlanta. We can stop there and eat, maybe look around for someplace to stay for a night."

Carla looked up. "You mean a motel?"

Brian took her by the shoulders. "Why not? It's far enough away that nobody will know us there. I'll tell you – one more night of sleeping on the ground and I'll be dead."

Carla laughed. "You're not kiddin' about that."

Brian took the sleeping bag from her. "Let's go."

4

Oak Creek was six hours away, according to Brian's guesswork. They would be there just after lunch.

The boy hadn't spoken a word to him since being caught trying to drive away. Drive – at his age! It was almost funny if you didn't think about how close the kid had come to getting away. It was like Carla had said – you couldn't really blame Shane for wanting to run away, but then you couldn't let him walk out, either. Something would have to change.

Shane's sudden, piercing voice made him jump. "Can I call my mom?"

Brian looked at him. "No."

"Why not?"

"Because."

"Can I write a letter?"

"No."

"Why not, Brian?" Carla asked. "He could at least let her know he's okay and all."

"No, dammit. He writes her a letter and she gets it and it's got Tennessee and Georgia postmarks all over it – no way. Use your brain."

"Oh, I forgot that." Carla turned to Shane. "Sorry, honey."

"Stop callin' me that."

Carla sucked in her breath. "Sorry."

Shane looked straight ahead, out the window. "Only my mom calls me that."

* * *

The day passed as a big blur. The road was constant motion with nothing to mark the time but the green exit signs. Atlanta slowed them down, but Brian was grateful for the break in the monotony. None of them spoke for several hours, and there was nothing but the static of the radio to pierce the silence. With her head against the passenger window, Carla dozed in the hot Georgia sun. A string of drool stretched from her lip to the collar of her t-shirt.

By the time the Oak Creek sign came into view, Brian's arms and legs were achy and stiff. Carla stirred as he slowed for the exit. "Where are we?"

"Just getting off the interstate at Oak Creek." He glanced at them. Shane looked straight ahead as if in a daze. Carla stretched and yawned. "You hungry?" he asked them.

"Starving," said Carla.

Oak Creek was small but not tiny. They spotted a restaurant right after they had crossed the source of the town's name, a swift muddy stream that looked like a white-water raft ride in an amusement park. "There!" Carla pointed. "Grandma's."

"Yeah, I see," said Brian. "But there's something we need to do before we eat." He began scanning the signs along the street. "Help me look for a used car place."

"Why?"

He sighed. "You'll find out – just look."

"Are you gonna trade cars?"

"No."

"There's one right up here on the left."

He finally saw it, just before he almost drove past it. Wilson Motors.

"They're closed," Carla said.

"I know," Brian said, pulling up between two rows of cars. He stepped out and folded down the seat, reaching behind it for a screwdriver.

"What're you gonna do?"

"Buy us a little bit of time." Brian squatted down behind the truck and unscrewed the license plate, then hid it under the pile of junk in the back. "We don't want to arouse any suspicion." He stepped over to one of the parked trucks and took the green-and-white plate off it carefully, then screwed it onto the back of his blue Ford. "There," he said. "Now nobody will have any reason to give us a second glance." He slid back into the seat. "Let's eat."

Carla smiled at him. "Sly, ain't ya?"

Brian put the truck into gear and headed back for the restaurant. "Damn straight."

Chapter 9

1

Shane was ravenous, though he tried not to show it. If he hadn't been so hungry he probably wouldn't have eaten; his cheeseburger was gristly and the fries were limp and tasteless. He tried not to show anything he felt. He hated it all – he hated Brian and he hated Carla, too. And it was easy to see that they didn't care much for him, either; all they were worried about was each other, and Shane was nothing but a big weight tied to both of them to slow down their progress.

There was only one thing he was grateful for, and that was the fact that he hadn't blacked out for a couple of days. There for awhile the spells had begun to come more frequently, and that had scared him. But now maybe they had stopped for good.

What really made him mad was that Brian wouldn't let him call home. Shane wanted so desperately to talk to his mother. But damned Brian had said no. Brian wouldn't even let him write a letter.

Brian had to have everything his way. If the restaurant hadn't been so crowded, Shane would have stabbed Brian right in the heart with the knife he was holding and cut him all the way down to his belly.

And he might have been able to eat in peace if the damned waitress hadn't been coming back every five minutes, asking them if everything was all right, if she could get them anything else, and all kinds of other bugshit. Even Shane realized all she wanted was a stupid tip, and he hoped silently that Brian wouldn't give her one.

His appetite taken care of, he sighed and laid his fork aside, content for a moment to just sit and look at the other people in the restaurant. Farmers, most of them, he guessed. And most were dressed up like they had just come from church.

Shane had never liked church because he always hated having to get dressed up and just sit there. And now he really felt sorry for a boy across the restaurant who was wearing a coat and a clip-on tie. He felt sorry for anybody who had to wear that many clothes in the summer, but this boy was crying. "Shut up," his mother said to him, clenching her napkin in the lap of her bright blue dress. "I'll whip you right here in front of all these people," she warned.

The boy howled louder and louder. "I hate you! I hate you!" he screamed suddenly, and was cut off the hard slap his mother gave him across the mouth.

Quickly, not wanting to stay in the sudden quiet of the restaurant, she whisked him up and headed for the door. A red-face man, presumable the father, made his way to the cash register to pay the check, and several of the other restaurant patrons gave low chuckles.

Brian laughed and looked across the table at Carla and Shane. "This looks like a real exciting place," he said.

Carla nodded, taking a sip of iced tea. "Yeah, it sure does."

Shane just looked away. He had seen little kids have tantrums before (and he had thrown plenty of them himself), but this one had utterly depressed him, and he didn't know why.

A dark-skinned man in a white t-shirt and a baseball cap stood and made his way toward the back of the restaurant. Shane's eyes followed the man's steps toward the restrooms. And he saw the pay-phone on the back wall, hidden in the little alcove next to the restroom doors.

Of course! All he had to do was ask to go to the restroom, then go and call his mother on a pay-phone. But then he realized that where they were sitting, Brian and Carla could see the phones by simply staring in a straight line; for Shane to pull off the plan, they would have to be on the other side of the restaurant. Besides, he didn't even have a quarter for the phone, and he sure couldn't ask Brian for one.

The man in the t-shirt was coming back. He stopped by the table where he had been sitting and dropped some change on it among the dirty dishes. Tips! Why hadn't he thought of that? All he had to do was swipe a quarter off one of the tables on his way to the phone. But he would have to be swift and sneaky. And he couldn't do it now anyway because of where they were sitting.

Dammit.

2

"What are we gonna do, Brian?" Carla asked, her gaze not moving from her plate.

"About what?"

"Everything. We can't keep runnin' forever."

"I know." He scratched at the beard stubble on his neck. "It's all so crazy. We'd be so much better off if we didn't have Shane," he said, meaning it.

Carla looked at him. "Have you thought about ransom? We could get enough money we might be set for life."

Brian shook his head. "I've thought about it. Only problem is that nobody ever gets it. We'd have to call his mother and tell her where to leave it and all, and as soon as we picked it up the cops would have us." He looked out the window at the parking lot. "I don't play them games."

"Have you thought of. . . just lettin' him go?"

Brian nodded. "Yeah. I just don't know about that."

"Then what're we gonna do with him?"

Brian looked at her, then at Shane, who never moved his eyes from whatever he was staring at across the restaurant. "I don't know."

3

By now Shane was getting used to motel rooms. The one they were in now was no better than any of the others, but at least its beds looked a little more comfortable. He flopped down on one of them now, exhausted from the previous night on the ground and the day's travels. "Can I go to sleep?"

"Yeah," Brian said. "That sounds like a good idea." He flipped on the television to a movie Shane remembered seeing the summer before. "Free cable," Brian said, grinning. He sat down on the other bed to watch it.

Shane rolled over and shut his eyes. The movie was a comedy, and every few minutes, Carla and Brian burst out laughing; Shane knew he would never get to sleep, but at least he could pretend. Then maybe they would leave him alone for awhile.

It still didn't seem possible that all this was happening. He was supposed to start school in a few days; what was he going to do if he was still with Brian and Carla? He would never see his friends again. They would all wonder what had happened to him; they might even think he was dead. And they would forget about him, just like they had forgotten about Randy Thomas, the boy that had moved away last year.

But what bothered him most was his mother. Where was she? Surely she was looking for him. If only he could call her. Maybe she thought he was dead and had already given up looking for him. He really didn't think she would just stop looking like that, but the more time went by he began to wonder. He remembered the first few days he had been with Brian, how he had wished every day for his mother to show up and take him home, how the wishes had turned into a faint longing, as if the desire to go home had diminished. He still wanted to be home more than ever, but he didn't cry about it anymore. He had come to realize over the past week that he couldn't just give up, that he would need hope and determination if he ever wanted to see his mother again.

* * *

Shane hadn't realized he had been asleep until the knock came at the door. He sat up, his vision blurry and his head aching, wondering if it had been real or if he had dreamed it. But Carla and Brian were getting up, too, alarm in their eyes, and he knew it was really happening.

Brian tip-toed to the window and peeked between the curtains. "Shit," he said, his face turning red. "It's a cop."

Behind Shane, Carla sucked in her breath. "What do we do?"

Brian glanced at her. "I guess we answer it. He knows we're in here, I'm sure." He stepped toward the door.

The policeman was tall with wisps of gray hair sticking out from under his cap. Shane's eyes went directly to the gun on the man's hip; it stuck out like a deformed appendage. "You own a blue Ford pickup?" he asked Brian.

Brian nodded, then swallowed. "Yeah. What's the problem?"

The cop motioned over his shoulder. "You're parked in front of a fire hydrant out here. I just happened to come by and I seen it."

Brian's shoulders fell with relief. "All right. I'll move it right now," he said, his voice shaky and breathless.

The door began to close. The cop was turning away. Shane knew he had to act fast, and he did. Suddenly, he was off the bed and heading for the door, screaming and screaming. He was trying to talk, but all his words were gibberish, unintelligible. He managed to get out "Wait!" and then Brian had him by the waist and was pulling him back, smiling at the cop's puzzled expression. "It's all right," Brian was saying. "He's retarded – he just gets excited."

The cop nodded in grim understanding, turning away.

"I'll move that truck in just a second," Brian told him. "Thanks." He shut the door and leaned against it, still holding Shane.

Carla was coming toward them. "God, that was close, Brian."

Brian nodded, his face slick with sweat, his chest rising and falling rapidly. He jerked Shane around in front of him. "You goddamn little shit!" he muttered.

Shane tried to brace himself for the blow he knew was coming, but he still wasn't prepared for it. It was full force against the side of his head, and he went reeling across the room, landing in a heap against the side of the bed.

"Brian!" Carla gasped.

"He damn near got us caught!" Brian said through his clenched teeth. "He damn near got us fucking caught!" He whirled around and stepped through the door, slamming it explosively behind him.

Carla knelt next to Shane. "Are you okay, honey? Shane?" He said nothing, sitting up and putting his head between his knees. "Are you gonna be sick?" Carla asked, smoothing back his hair. "You don't understand," she said. "You can't do this. You can't get us caught. You just can't."

Shane stared at the floor and sobbed.

* * *

With some luck, Shane was able to persuade Brian and Carla to eat at Grandma's Restaurant again that night. They reluctantly agreed, and Shane was ecstatic – his plan was working!

Once inside, he led the way toward the far wall of the place. "Why do you want to sit all the way over here?" Brian asked.

Shane just shrugged, sliding into the booth. He couldn't believe he was actually leading them into this. They were letting him trap them. He almost felt sorry for them.

The waitress came and brought the menus. Shane pretended to study his, but he was so nervous about his plan that he could barely read it. He finally ordered a grilled cheese and a coke. He hoped Brian and Carla didn't see how badly he was shaking.

Brian turned to Carla and his voice made Shane jump. "How about we head down to Florida in the morning?"

Carla's mouth dropped open. "Florida! What is there in Florida?"

"Jobs for one thing," Brian said. "I knew a guy that went down there for a week and got three job offers right out of the blue."

"Really?"

Brian looked at her. "You ever been there?"

She shook her head. "No. This is the first time I was ever out of Kentucky."

Brian laughed. "You're kidding."

"Nope," she said, smiling.

"Well, I was eight years old before I knew there was a world outside of Indiana."

Behind Brian's head, Shane could see two people leaving the next table, and he craned his neck anxiously. The man was helping the lady out of the booth. He dug into his pocket and laid some change under a napkin. Shane's heart began to pound. Here it was – the opportunity he had been waiting for.

"I gotta use the bathroom," he said, vaguely aware he had interrupted Brian in mid-sentence.

Brian sighed and looked at him. "All right, let's go." He started to get up.

"No," Shane said. "I mean, can't I go by myself? You never give me any privacy."

"I'm not letting you go anywhere alone," Brian told him.

"Come on, Brian," Carla said. "He can't go anywhere else. Look." She pointed toward the restroom alcove. "We can see him when he comes out."

Brian sighed again. "Okay. But if you're not back in five minutes, I'm coming after you."

Shane scurried across Carla's lap and out of the booth. He stopped directly in front of the next table, slipping into the booth. "Brian?" His hands, hidden by the back of the seat, searched beneath the napkin behind him as the man turned around. "Thanks," he told him and grabbed the coins. The he scrambled toward the restrooms.

In the dark corner he unclenched his quaking hands and found three quarters and two dimes. He had never made a collect call before, so he popped in a quarter and dialed the operator.

"Operator," a female voice said instantly.

"I want to make a collect call to Liz Robinson in Cranston, Indiana," he told her.

"Number, please?"

"Area code 812, 555-7453," he said proudly, glad his parents had made him memorize his phone number.

"Could I have your name, please?"

"Shane Robinson."

"Okay, Shane, just a moment."

"Please hurry," he said. He hopped up and down. What if Brian decided to come back here anyway? What if he popped around the corner right now?

The phone began to ring on the other end. It rang three times before his mother finally answered. "Hello?" she said, and Shane thought he would cry.

"I have a collect call from Shane Robinson," the operator said. "Will you accept?"

"Yes!" his mother screamed. "Shane? Is that you."

"Hi, Mom," he said, and his eyes began to water.

"Oh, my God! Where are you?"

"Georgia."

"Are you all right? Did he hurt you?"

"Listen," Shane said. "They don't know I'm callin', so I have to be quick. We're in Oak Creek and we're stayin' at the Oak Creek Inn. We're in room eighteen. I think we're leaving for Florida in the morning."

"Okay," his mother said. "Oh, my God! Are you all right?"

"Yeah," he said. "How's Bowser?"

His mother laughed but he could tell she was crying, too. "Bowser is just fine, honey. We'll have you safe as soon as possible."

"Okay," Shane said, the tears flowing freely now. "'Bye."

He hung up the phone and stared at it for a minute. Then he wiped his eyes and went back to the table. They didn't even look at him as he slid into his seat.

Chapter 10

1

As soon as Liz had picked the phone back up to call the police, her own words came flooding back to her.

  . . . I would love to take a gun and blow that bastard away.

  . . . I'd like to splatter his blood all over the state.

  . . . nothin' they can do to justify what he did.

She placed the receiver gently back into its cradle and looked at it. Half of her wanted to do the right thing, to pick up the phone and call the police and let them take care of it. But the rest of her, some part deep within her, was savage. She wanted that man dead – more than she had ever wanted anything in her life. He didn't deserve to live. He had killed her husband, taken Dan Turner's wife, and had her son and only God knew what else.

She straightened. Dan Turner. He said something last night about wanting to go after the bastard himself. But was he serious or merely joking? She had to know, and there was no denying what she had to do.

She ran for her purse and pawed through it until she found Dan Turner's phone number, scrawled on the back of an old bank receipt. Would he agree or would he think she was just crazy, an overreacting mother wanting to go off on some vigilante killing spree? She punched in the number, her heart slamming against her ribs. *No, no, no!* she told herself as the phone on the other end began to ring. Why was she doing this? Why wasn't she right now dialing the police?

"Hello?"

"Mr. Turner? This is Liz Robinson." She swallowed. "I – I just heard from Shane."

"He call ya?"

"Yes. Just now. He said they were in Oak Creek, Georgia. Do you know where that is?"

"Yeah. Right outside Atlanta. Did you call the law?"

"Not yet." She swallowed again, hard. "Were you serious about what you said last night?"

"I don't know. What did I say last night?"

She frowned. "You know – about wanting to go after that son-of-a-bitch."

He was silent for a moment on the other end. "Why?"

God, she thought. Dan Turner wasn't making this any easier. "Because if you were, I'm ready to go down there with you."

Dan Turner laughed. "Oh, now I see. You wanna go traipsin' off down there so you can kill him, is that it? Then he'll be dead and you'll have your satisfaction that he got what he deserved."

Liz's mouth dropped open. She shut it. Dan had guessed it all.

"Only thing I can't figure out is why you want me to go? You seem like you could take care of him yourself."

"I need you to help me."

"I know what you want," his far-away voice said. "You want me to go with you so I can kill him, and you won't have blood on your hands."

"No!" she gasped, knowing full well that had been her intention all along. "That's not exactly it."

"Well, ain't it?"

"No." She cleared her throat. "The way I look at it, he's got my son and your wife; we need to work together to get them out."

He was silent, contemplating it, she guessed. "It's gonna be dangerous, you know," he said.

"Yes. I know."

He was quiet for a moment. "All right."

Liz let out her breath. "Then you'll do it?"

"Yeah. But only on one condition. I want you to understand somethin'. We go by my rules."

Liz stood. "Wait. What rules?"

"Listen a minute, will ya?" He sighed. "First of all, we use my plan. I already got somethin' figured out – I'll tell you about it in a minute. Second, you've got to promise me the cops won't ever know about any of this. What we're discussin' here."

"Okay. I promise."

"Good. Now, the last thing. . . "

"Yes?"

"The last thing is, once all this is through, we don't keep in touch."

"All right."

"Good. Now the first thing you gotta do is come down and pick me up. Then we'll head on down to Georgia."

"Mr. Turner, thank you."

"You bet."

* * *

In the station wagon, Liz studied the atlas briefly, seeing just how far she was from Dan Turner, and then how far she was from Shane. It was three hundred miles to Macon City and another three hundred to Oak Creek. Six hundred miles. She glanced at her watch. If she kept her speed constant, she could be with Shane in the morning.

If she kept her speed constant.

She pulled down the driveway and headed for Cranston, her body numb. Nothing in the past couple of weeks seemed real. Everything she had done had been in a fog, a dream. She supposed it must be a kind of shock. That mixed with the tense agony of losing Mitchell and then waiting by the phone day after day, night after night to hear from the police or Shane would have been enough to drive her crazy if she had let it. She didn't know what she would have done if Shane had been found dead. But now she knew he was alive, and nothing was going to stop her from getting him. And that bastard would pay. He would pay dearly.

* * *

The rain hit right as Liz crossed over the border into Kentucky. It started gradually, but by the time she had gone ten miles into the state, the wind was blowing the downpour against the windshield, and she had to pull off the road for about fifteen minutes.

When she finally drove back onto the four-lane, the radio station she was picking up was calling for more rain and a tornado watch until nine o'clock. Great.

It was night now. Sunset had come as dull and colorless as a stone. She stopped for gas and pulled out the map as she waited, dismayed at finding that she was only halfway to Macon City. The rain had definitely slowed her progress. She had been on the road for nearly three hours, and now she was fifty miles behind.

"Some weather we're havin'," the attendant said from under the hood of his plastic slicker.

"Yes," she answered, handing him a twenty-dollar bill.

"This is the worst storm we've had all summer."

"Would have to happen tonight."

"What's that?" he called over the wind.

Liz cleared her throat. "I said it looks like it'll last all night."

He nodded at her, his eyes squinting behind thick, water-spotted glasses. "Yeah. Radio says there's tornado watches out, so you be careful."

"I will," she smiled. "I really will."

* * *

She reached Dan Turner's at twelve-thirty.

It had stopped raining about an hour before, and she had been able to catch up some of her lost time, increasing her speed about fifteen miles an hour over the limit, praying all the while she wouldn't get a ticket.

Dan Turner stepped off the porch as she opened her door. "You're late," he said.

"I know. I got caught in a big storm right after I crossed the state line."

He knelt beside the rear of the car. "I'm gonna give you some gas."

"No, you don't have to do that. I'll pay for it."

He was shaking his head. "Nope. It's on me."

Liz decided not to press it. The tank was almost empty, and she hadn't thought to bring much cash with her. "Thanks."

He grunted. "Least I can do."

They said nothing else until they were back on the interstate, edging closer to Tennessee. Liz could take the silence no longer. "Mr. Turner?"

"Please. Dan."

"Dan – do you think we're doing the right thing?"

He sighed. "All I know is, he's gonna pay for what he did, and lockin' him up for two or three years ain't gonna do it."

"You're right about that." She sighed, still uncertain. "I just hope God forgives me."

He looked at her. "I hope God forgives all of us."

Lightning flashed to the south.

2

In the dim light that filtered through the curtains, Carla could see that Shane was asleep on the other bed, his feet and hands tied to the legs of the bedframe.

Silently, she deftly slid astride Brian's hips and felt him respond. "He's asleep," she whispered.

"Are you sure?"

"Yeah."

They made love, trying to keep as quiet as possible, and when it was over, Carla lay in the crook of his arm, smiling to herself in the darkness. This was all she had ever wanted, she thought. Tomorrow they would begin their drive to Florida, and no one would stop them. No one would know they were there, and no one would care. Brian could get a job and they could get an apartment or maybe even a house. Shane didn't bother her anymore; she figured she could persuade Brian to let him go before they crossed the state line. Just let him loose in the middle of nowhere, and they would be long gone before anyone found him.

Outside, thunder rolled across the sky, but Carla was safe in Brian's arms. And as the rain moved in, she drifted off to sleep.

3

It had stopped raining by the time Dan and Liz reached Oak Creek and the first gray light of dawn was creeping into the eastern sky. The town was dead. Only the streets, warm and wet and steaming, seemed to be alive.

"Where'd you say they were stayin'?" Dan asked.

"Oak Creek Inn."

He could tell she was nervous, and somehow that amused him. "Calm down. There ain't nothin' to worry about."

She glared at him. "I just wonder if we're making a big mistake. Maybe we should have just called the police."

He shook his head. "We both know why we didn't do that, so there's no sense in dwellin' on it."

"But I still think – "

"There it is." Dan pointed toward a glowing sign. Blue neon water flowed underneath the pink words OAK CREEK INN. "Vacancy" flashed on and off in bright red.

Liz slowed the station wagon to a creep. "What do we do now?"

He scanned the highway. "Pull up to that restaurant there and let me out."

"Then what're you going to do?"

"Don't you worry about it."

Liz swung into the parking lot of Grandma's Restaurant and turned off the engine. "I don't like this."

He looked at her and ran a hand down his stubbly face. "Sorry." He opened the door. "You stay here 'til you see me standing on the parkin' lot of the motel. Then wait five minutes and go call the police." He pointed to a gas station half a block away. "I see a pay phone up there."

"Call the police?"

"Just do as I say." He opened the door. "What room you say it was?"

"Eighteen."

He started to step out, but Liz caught his sleeve and looked him in the eyes. "One thing," she said. "Anything happens to Shane and I will hunt you down. I swear to God."

He gave her a humorless smile. "I know you will."

He shut the door behind him and started walking up the side of the highway, not taking his eyes off the neon sign. Inside the pocket of his parka he clutched the only thing that made him feel safe – his pistol.

A car approached him, its lights on bright. He pulled his cap down over his eyes and stared at the edge of the highway, wondering if it was the cops. The old brown Buick passed, and he sighed with relief.

Now, in front of the motel, he crossed the highway and stood in the hazy, flashing glow of the humming sign, looking down the road toward the station wagon. Liz flashed the brake lights, and he smiled.

Turning back toward the motel, he spotted Hamby's truck at once. It had a Georgia plate on it, but there was no mistaking that faded blue color. And his eyes had no trouble finding room eighteen.

As he walked toward the door, he was unaware that he was still smiling.

4

In the fog of sleep, Brian was first only vaguely aware of a pounding noise. But then Carla was suddenly shaking him. "Brian!" she whispered. "Brian! Wake up! Somebody's at the door!"

"Shut up," he moaned. "It's just the thunder."

"No! Somebody's there!"

The pounding came again, and this time, Brian came fully awake, his heart pounding in his chest. "Oh, shit!" He jumped out of bed and stepped into his jeans. He looked over to see Carla already dressed. Shane was beginning to stir. "You keep that boy quiet."

He made his way to the window in the darkness, scraping his shin on a chair. Gingerly he lifted the curtain and peeked out. Someone was there, all right, but he couldn't make out the shadowy face.

"Who is it?" Carla whispered.

"I don't know. I can't tell." He stepped toward the door. "Who's there?" he called.

"Police. Open up."

Carla turned on the light and brightness flooded the room. "Oh, God, Brian! What do we do?"

Brian looked around frantically, trying to remember where the gun was. He spotted it on the bedside table. "Take those ropes off Shane," he said. "Hide the gun." The pounding came again as Carla struggled with the knots. "Just a minute!" Brian yelled.

Carla's fingers were bleeding by the time she had loosened the last rope, and she was crying, nearly hysterical. Brian looked at Shane. "You sit there on the edge of that bed, boy, and don't you move." He turned around and unlocked the door, then opened it.

It wasn't until after Carla had screamed that he realized what he was looking at: He was standing face to face with Dan Turner, the man she had killed. Dan Turner with a gun in his hand and an eerie grin on his face.

Turner cocked the pistol. "You miserable sonvabitch."

Before he could stop himself, Brian grabbed Shane off the bed and held the boy in front of him. Shane gave a startled cry and began to whimper. "You can't do this to me," Brian yelled at Dan. "The cops'll have your ass before you're even out of town."

"Dan!" Carla pleaded. "Stop it! Stop it!"

But Dan didn't look at her. He was backing Brian into the corner of the room.

And then, for no reason at all, the boy in Brian's hands was shaking – shaking violently, as if he were having some sort of seizure. Shane was sinking down to the floor, his glassy eyes rolling back into his head. Brian glanced up at Dan and he felt his bowels loosen.

Dan pulled the trigger.

5

When Shane was first waking up, the only thing he knew was that he was in bed. But then he saw Dan Turner slide open the bedside table drawer and pull out the pistol Brian had stolen from Shane's father. Dan picked it up with his hands wrapped in his shirttail. He saw Shane looking at him. "Hold your ears, kid," he said. Shane stuck his fingers in his ears just as Dan Turner shot his own leg. The tall, blond man went down on his knees, clutching his left leg as it spurted blood.

Then Shane saw Brian on the floor, his eyes wide open and unseeing, blood and gore smeared all over his bare chest, and Shane knew the man was dead. Dan crawled toward the body and carefully put the gun in Brian's hand, mashing the fingers against the butt and trigger, then let it fall by the dead man's head. Shane looked away, hugging his head into his pillow.

He was barely aware that somewhere in the room, Carla was whimpering softly. He looked up and spotted her crouched in a corner, her face hidden in her hands.

Dan slipped off his parka and then writhed out of his t-shirt and wrapped it around the wound. The white material was soon a bright red. He edged his way toward Shane and sank down onto the bed beside him. "I want you to listen to me," he said. "if you wanna go home an' be back with your mama, for God's sake listen to me."

"I'm listenin'," Shane whispered.

"When the police ask you what happened, here's what you tell 'em: I knocked on the door an' he answered it. I came in here, and when he saw it was me, he shot me. He picked you up to use you as a shield, only you had some kind of attack or somethin' and he dropped you. That's when I shot him. Okay?"

Shane nodded.

"All right."

Shane motioned toward Carla. "What about her? Won't she tell?"

Dan shook his head. "She won't be sayin' nothin' to anybody."

Shane leaned against Dan's shoulder, and Dan hugged him.

Off in the distance, the sirens began.

6

Liz's heart was pounding like a bass drum in her chest. The police still wouldn't let her into the room, and she knew something horrible had happened. An ambulance had come and they had just brought out the body of a man. The sheet on top of him was blood-soaked. Whether it was Dan Turner or the other man she didn't know. She stood with her gaze frozen on the open door of the room. She was still amazed at how many people were here. Some were motel guests, still in their pajamas and robes. But a few, it looked to her, had driven out here from their homes just to witness the grisly goings-on.

There was a tap on her shoulder. "Ma'am?"

She turned and found herself facing a police officer. "Yes?"

"Your son is just fine."

She burst into tears and sank against him. "Oh, thank God, thank God." She wiped her eyes and looked back at him. "Can I see him now?"

"No, not yet. He's still bein' questioned. Accordin' to what we know so far," he said, "Mr. Turner knocked on the door and was met by Mr. DeCanto – "

"DeCanto?" The name sounded vaguely familiar.

"Yes, ma'am. Brian DeCanto. We found an Indiana driver's license on the body."

Liz took a deep breath. "Body. Then that was him they just brought out."

"Yes, ma'am. Apparently, Mr. DeCanto fired at Mr. Turner and wounded him in the leg, but he's all right. Then Mr. DeCanto picked up your son to use him as a shield, but the boy had some kind of attack and Mr. DeCanto dropped him. Then Mr. Turner fired at Mr. DeCanto and killed him."

Liz was still trying to comprehend it all. "Did you say Shane had some kind of attack?"

The officer nodded. "Yes, ma'am. One of the paramedics checked him over and thinks there might be a possibility he had an epileptic seizure."

"Seizure?"

"It was very mild, but I think that when you get home he should see a doctor."

Liz nodded. "Yes, of course." She turned away, then looked back. "Thank you – I – I don't even know your name."

The man smiled a large, easy grin. "Chief Adams, ma'am."

Liz smiled back. "Thanks, Chief."

She started to say something else, but then she caught sight of a small figure being led outside by two more officers. "Shane!" She flew across the parking spaces toward him. One of her shoes took flight and landed beneath a car.

"Mom!"

They caught each other, and she hugged him like she had never hugged anyone before. She pressed his little body so close to her that she thought she would break his ribs, and she burst into tears again instead. "Oh, God, are you all right?"

"Uh-huh."

She smelled the odor of his sweat-soaked hair and thanked God for it, then held him away so she could look at him. "I missed you so much, honey."

"I missed you, too," he whispered. Tears flowed down his cheeks in dirty streaks.

Behind him, Dan Turner, his bleeding leg bandaged, was brought out on a stretcher by two paramedics. Liz glanced up at him and mouthed,

"Thank you." He nodded at her as the paramedics moved on toward the waiting ambulance.

"Mom? Can we go home now?"

She hugged him again. "Yes, honey."

She picked him up, heavy as he was, and carried him through the maze of people and whirling lights.

June

Carla sat silently in the lawn chair on the sunny front porch of Turner's Gas & Groceries. Her belly was swollen grotesquely with Brian DeCanto's child, but Dan – stupid, ignorant Dan – thought it was his. He had raped her the next night – the night after he had killed Brian – and now he thought she was carrying his child. But Carla knew the truth. Somehow she just knew.

Dan stepped around the corner of the building and eyed her forever. Then he limped inside.

I will kill him after the baby comes, she thought. I will do it then. It's only a few more days. Then I will do it.

She sighed and watched the dust rise with the heat from the roadway.

If not now, then in August.

www.ingramcontent.com/pod-product-compliance
Lightning Source LLC
Chambersburg PA
CBHW052142170626
46812CB00004B/1552